ANGELINO HEIGHTS

Angelino Heights

ADAM BREGMAN

Author

N

NewPlainsPress.com

First Printing, 2020

Published by Agreement with
Summerfield Publishing,
New Plains Press
Auburn, AL 36831

ISBN 13: 978-1-7345719-4-3

Bregman, Adam 1971–

To my wife, editor and proofreader, Federica Santini, with immense love for your invaluable contributions to this novel.

CONTENTS

~ 1 ~

BOULEVARD OF DREAMS

"I feel perfectly square identifying myself as an Angeleno. It is here amidst cool ocean breezes, greasy churros, and psychedelic sunsets that I'm in my element, where my heart is at peace. Not only do I feel affection toward L.A. institutions like Angelyne and the triangle offense, I also have a soft spot for some of the dingier aspects of the city: far-flung thrift stores and pawn shops that beckon few customers, dumpy neighborhood Thai restaurants lacking the slightest ambience, the broken neon signs of old businesses that have disappeared.

From the point of view of Easterners who live in snow-covered metropolises, Angelenos are at times perceived to be trim, laid-back, suntanned jerkoffs, which is perhaps only the case if you compare them to your average New Yorker. More commonly, Angelenos are just as high-strung, ripping their hair out over the height of a neighbor's fence or dog poop on their lawn. Though it's not like Manhattan where a laundry closet rents for $3000 a month, Los Angeles has also become a pricey place to live with few who can afford to spend their week lounging at the beach.

Some years ago, rather suddenly, I realized I was smitten with this city, even if it has at times been cruel to me. My infatuation with Los Angeles extends to woeful streets like Washington Boulevard in Pasadena or Glenoaks Boulevard in Glendale, which make me sentimental for the time I've spent wandering them. Wide boulevards strewn with gloomy mini-malls comprised of random businesses that have nothing to do with each other, like a Filipino fast food chain bookended by an Armenian-owned copy shop and a vacuum cleaner repair store, are as emblematic of Los Angeles as Fernando Valenzuela. To go along with my fondness for arbitrary ethnic crapola, I also strongly believe in the preservation of every dated piece of architecture in the city from rotting Sixties-era motels painted brown and orange to forlorn diners with abundant character and tasteless food. As long as it is antiquated and of Los Angeles, it should remain standing. In past decades, this city has been unkind to its history, bulldozing the Victorian homes that once graced Bunker Hill and tearing down almost every branch of the Brown Derby in Hollywood. At Disneyland, the old Tomorrowland, once a cute, kitschy, Jetsons-like vision of the future, was replaced by generic attractions that evoke neither a tangible, nor an imagined tomorrow. It's not that I'm opposed to change. It's just that I prefer they don't change anything, unless it's somehow for the better.

As an L.A. native, I also have informed and unyielding opinions regarding Mexican food. Guacamole should have a little kick to it. It shouldn't taste like sour cream. Tacos should be rolled in corn tortillas and the flavor should be uncomplicated and require few ingredients. Burritos involve meat, cheese, onions and salsa, maybe rice and beans, possibly guacamole or pico de gallo. But you can't just shove anything in there and call it a burrito. If there is spinach or grilled vegetables or an organic, oddly-colored tortilla holding it all, that is a wrap, something hippies and yoga teachers eat, not a burrito, something Angelenos subsist on. Good Mexican food is served at taquerias or from taco trucks all over L.A. You can find exceptional taco trucks almost everywhere, even camped out in fancy neighborhoods, where they serve construction workers, say in the deepest reaches of Orange County. When Mexican food is served in anything called a restaurant, it may be suspect. While there are many fine Mexican restaurants in L.A. serving fantastic mariscos and delicious homemade tortillas, most in L.A., and for that matter, the rest of the world, serve a perverted cuisine consisting of flaming fajitas, malevolent cheese sauce, and sugary margaritas, which has as much to do with true Mexican food as Barry Manilow.

My politics are also utterly Angeleno or Californian in that I'm your typical Democrat and supporter of liberal causes. I believe in taxing the rich and what have you. I'm opposed to wars in far-off countries for questionable gains and the like. It's all half-assed on my part in that I rarely lift a finger. I mean I vote, I blab sometimes, but not much else. If Californians come up with some odd idea such as banning salad dressings or outlawing smoking in canoes, I'm likely to go along with it because I'm wired in the same vaguely progressive manner as the rest of them. Angelenos aren't necessarily about to let transgendered ferrets run the economy like San Franciscans might propose, but they do conjure up ideas that appear nutso to much of the rest of the country. I support this endeavor to try to drag the stodgy heartland of America toward some unobtainable liberal ideal.

And while I am as proud as Cheech Marin to be a native-born Angeleno, I don't subscribe to any sort of American flag waving or patriotic bullshit-mongering. America is not the best country in the world, though it's a little more dynamic than Belgium. Overseas, America is often associated with militarism, Big Macs, capital punishment, and sappy romantic comedies, none of which I would ever endeavor to defend. It's as if Los Angeles exists outside of America in some other country, where non-fat yogurt and pet psychiatrists rule as opposed to country ham and scrapbooking."

Removed for a moment from his fervently expressed rant, Nathan Lyme glanced at the person to whom he had been speaking. Claudia, the girl with whom he had recently been spending time, had been listening to him with one ear as they sauntered next to the bluffs of Point Fermin Park in San Pedro, not too far from where she lived in a tiny hovel in Long Beach.

Three weeks before, in the incandescent early autumn of the year 1997, at the *Mutiny on the Bounty* themed Wilshire Boulevard bar, the HMS Bounty, Nathan had spotted her, a fanciful girl with bulging eyeballs and a shiny, prominently sculptured nose, drinking with her friend seated at a brown upholstered booth below decorative portholes. With nail polish stains on the sleeves of her leather biker jacket, Claudia was the sort of party girl Nathan could pick out of a lineup.

A little bored with how things were progressing with her, he dropped Claudia off at her pad, politely said farewell, tipping an imaginary hat in her direction, and headed back to Hollywood on the Harbor Freeway, stopping at what he called the hipster Trader Joe's in Silver Lake. As Nathan perused the cheap Italian wine section, he noticed an extremely talkative, middle-aged character with thick eyeglasses and curly, orangish hair who resembled an older and paunchier version of Gene Wilder, striking up conversations with everyone in the store. An employee who was handing out chicken tamale samples was cornered.

"Have you ever been to a Dodgers game?" the man asked the smiley young girl who was cooking tamales.

"No."

"You really should go some time. People say baseball is boring, but to me it's like poetry. Not everyone can appreciate its serene and comforting qualities. Things may move slowly, but they move at their own deliberate pace. No one's in a hurry. Dodger Stadium in Elysian Park is great: Farmer John hot dogs, regulars there every game, daily sunshine, and fireworks at night. It's an experience. It's not about the games. The Dodgers lose half the time. What about the movies? Do you go to the movies?"

"I usually watch movies at home with my boyfriend," said the girl.

"You know, I went to Cornell in the Fifties, but then I came out to L.A. because I really wanted to make it as a screenwriter. I sold a couple of scripts, none of them were made into films. So, I got into the music business, worked for A&M, RCA for a while. Ever heard of The Seeds?"

"No, I haven't," said the girl sounding perky.

"I discovered them playing in some dump. Eventually, I got into music publishing and then radio promotion. What do you listen to?"

"Oh, everything," said the girl, "I like samba, pop, rock en español, bossa nova, you name it."

"I love playing tennis. It keeps me fit. I've been playing every Sunday with the same partner for the last fifteen years. These tamales are delicious!"

While Nathan filled his shopping basket, he witnessed the man conversing with everyone in the store and at one point dancing with an employee to an Elton John song they were playing over the store's speakers.

"Nut job," thought Nathan. "There's no way to avoid it. He's going to talk to me."

Before he could make it to the checkout line, the man suddenly appeared next to him in the vitamins section.

"Did you see that story in the *Times* today about the Yoshinoya Beef Bowl murders?"

"Didn't read the paper today," replied Nathan.

"Some guy has been going around to Yoshinoya Beef Bowls in the middle of the night and quietly murdering random patrons by shooting them in the back of the head with a silencer and then dropping their head into their noodle bowls. The corpse they found last night had been sitting there for a half hour before someone came into the place, noticed him and called the only employee, who had been in the back the whole time on the phone. That's crazy, ha? Three guys have been found killed the same way at two different Yoshinoya Beef Bowls. I guess it serves them right for eating at that place."

"It's the risk you take," said Nathan.

"Ha!" replied the man.

Returning to the unassuming, minimally decorated duplex that he rented on Talmadge Street in Los Feliz, Nathan contemplated what he might want to do that Friday night. One option was a party being thrown by a friend of a friend named Zach, an overly handsome guy who was the sort who sported a pseudo beard of stubble to look manlier. Their mutual friend, Anders, really more of an acquaintance who Nathan had met at the coffeehouse, the Bourgeois Pig, had sent him an email invite. Based on Zach's address and his ostensible likability, Nathan assumed Zach lived in a fancy pad, probably a house in Hancock Park, and would throw a decent party.

Glancing out his window, Nathan noticed his odd neighbor, Ed, walking his dog. The schnauzer was sniffing about, contemplating the diversity of scents on the duplex lawn. Nathan had been awestruck the morning previous when he had witnessed Ed running down the street in his blue and white striped pajamas, chasing the trash truck.

"You missed my can! You missed my can!" Ed had exhorted the garbage man when he caught up with him.

"Oh man, I did! Sorry about that. I'll swing the truck around," replied the mystified garbage man.

"Yeah, well, I got a lot of garbage today," said Ed, catching his breath.

Ed caught Nathan eyeing him from his window, waved uneasily and moved along.

When Nathan arrived at Zach's classy, Spanish style home with its red-tiled roof, on Rossmore Avenue, everything at the party was much as he had imagined. Making his way through the crowded living room packed mostly with girls having loud conversations, he spotted Zach, who clearly did not recognize him, even though he nodded in his direction. Then came a tap on his shoulder. It was Anders, wearing a gold dinner jacket, which perhaps he should not have been wearing, and his girlfriend, Elena, with a bountiful head of hair and a toothy smile, who Anders introduced to him.

"Nathan and I met while playing a game of pool," Anders explained to Elena.

"I didn't know you played pool," replied Elena.

"Normally, that's not something I do. But Nathan here can play."

"My father taught me how to play pool," recalled Nathan. "I think I was eight years old. He knew every trick. In his day, women were not allowed in pool halls because it was a game that attracted some rough customers. I liked to play it when I was a layabout teenager."

He decided against mentioning that his dad was an actual, part-time pool shark, who sometimes came home with a fair take from the game and that he had passed on all the knowledge he could to his son.

"Nathan, I can't remember, what do you do?" asked Anders curiously.

A perennial question that nagged Nathan and which he seemed to be asked continuously when he went out on the town was what he did for a living. He had pondered if this query was as characteristic of Los Angeles as he.

"I work in post-production, mostly TV, video editing, that sort of thing," said Nathan using his standard answer. It seemed that many in the late Nineties in L.A. were in this profession, so it suited Nathan just fine as a cover, even if he knew next to nothing about the job.

"Shall we get something to drink?" asked Nathan.

"Do you like fancy, artisan root beer?" replied Anders.

"I guess," replied Nathan, "though I was thinking a cocktail or wine."

"Not going to happen, my fine feathered friend. All that's available in that kitchen is fancy soda, bubbly water, and bottled iced tea. This party is strictly sober."

"Sober?" replied Nathan befuddled.

"You didn't know Zach was in the program? A lot of the folks here are AA, and likely most of these loose looking gals," explained Anders, as Elena shot him a look. "When you walked in, did you notice how many people were smoking out front? Way too many. Nobody smokes anymore but teenagers, right? AA types are chain smokers. I'm sorry that I didn't mention it was a sober party in my email. I forgot."

Nathan looked around a tad bewildered.

"I admit, had I known, I wouldn't have shown up," said Nathan.

Disheartened, he settled on a Thomas Kemper Root Beer and plotted whether to ditch the party. But then another idea grabbed him and propelled him upstairs, which was deserted, and into a bedroom, where he found, as he suspected he might, a pile of coats and some purses belonging to partygoers downstairs piled on a bed. With just a second's hesitation, he ripped open the first purse, finding a wallet, $10, a credit card, nothing else. He rifled through a second purse, which was hidden under the bed, a couple hundred bucks, three credit cards, a bracelet with several topazes, maybe gold, definitely worth something. Tossing the purse aside, he went through the pockets of the coats. Nothing. His eyes darted around the room noticing an antique clock, way too cumbersome, but likely more valuable than everything else he had nabbed.

Then, unmistakably, he heard someone coming up the steps. He went behind the door. A skinny fellow with a ratty blonde beard appeared in front of him. He picked up his coat. Nathan could tell he sensed his presence behind the door. Before the unlucky fellow could turn around, Nathan threw a roundhouse punch, clocking him on the back of the head and sending him sprawling on top of the coats. The guy then rolled over the bed in slow motion like a downed soldier in a dramatic death scene in a war film and collapsed into the small space on the floor next to the dresser. Confident that he was out cold, Nathan collected himself. The fall on the floor had been loud, but the party downstairs was noisier.

He walked out of the room and down the stairs at a normal pace, breathing slowly and gathering a sense of poise, so as to react quickly and assuredly, no matter what happened next. To not appear as a suspect when the police arrived later, he thought it best to seek out Anders and Elena and say goodbye. He thought he might have a few minutes before the knocked out dude was discovered or came to and were he found sooner, he felt he could beat it out of there before the police were called.

Picking up the root beer he had left on a coffee table, he took a swig.

"I think I am going to head to a bar," said Nathan calmly to Anders. "The sober party concept is just not for me."

"I understand," replied Anders. "We would join you, except Zach is a pal and I feel I need to hang out longer to show support for his temperate lifestyle. Thanks for showing up man."

Nathan found his black Audi A4 several blocks away and drove off, debating whether to use the credit cards right away at a liquor store in Hollywood on Fountain Avenue nearby, where a youngish Bangladeshi fellow worked who rarely asked for an ID. He might have an hour or two or perhaps more before the credit cards were called in as stolen, especially with everybody at the party being sober. At the traffic light of Santa Monica Boulevard and Vine Street, he counted the cash, $245.

"What a pathetic score," he thought, "the risk so outweighed the spoils. That poor fellow, who is only guilty of showing up at a lame party, is going to the hospital with a concussion so I can have a few extra bucks to toss around."

He then recalled the bracelet and began digging around in his pockets. At the next stoplight, he gave it a look, white gold with four medium-sized topaz stones. He liked the look of it, envisioning something in the range of $400 and realized that it was likely a decent take in the end, considering the circumstances. Now, far away from the party, he felt that he had evaded any trouble.

Tossing the credit cards out the window, Nathan turned on to Los Feliz Boulevard in the direction of one of his favorite hangouts, The Roost, an aging dive bar in Atwater Village, which a youthful crowd had recently transformed into a happening spot. Turning on the radio and finding the *BBC News*, he began to unwind, rubbing the stones of the bracelet in his jacket pocket, and in minutes put all that had transpired behind him.

~ 2 ~

UNDER DIM LIGHT

In the parking lot, on the residential sidewalk on the way to the Roost, at the door of the bar and now just inside the door of the bar, Audrey, Dalton Everest's date for the evening, had bumped into friends and acquaintances, exchanging pleasantries and local art scene gossip. The owner of a contemporary art gallery and an unapologetic, full time schmooze, Audrey appeared to know every person even loosely associated with the art or music crowd in Los Angeles.

"It's too bad Audrey is a Bozo magnet," considered Dalton while fingering his bellybutton. "For the most part, I like hanging out with her. But I don't understand the urge to be friends with every Tom, Dick, and Harry."

They had just come from a trendy Asian fusion restaurant on Melrose, which Audrey had suggested, and where at two separate tables she had spotted guys whom she knew (both über-bland) and had gone over to chat with them, dragging along Dalton, who had grown up in the obscure, dull San Fernando Valley suburb of Arleta and had never bumped into someone he knew in a restaurant.

"Audrey, do you remember Weasel?" asked a stout, pretentious-looking fellow who approached them at the Roost.

"Of course." replied Audrey. "What's Weasel been up to?"

"I got a hold of his new number. He lives in Huntington Beach. I think he's given up performance. He's married and has a daughter. For a while, he's been trying to get me to drive down to Huntington Beach and see him. But you know, it's far. He's always saying it's not far. So, the other night, I call him because I'm going to an opening in Long Beach and I say maybe I can swing by because it's kind of close to him, and he gets all offended that I am not coming down there to see him specifically, that I am just fitting it into my schedule. He basically says don't bother."

Dalton chuckled at this story.

"I always thought Weasel would become the next Klaus Nomi," said Audrey. "Milo, this is my friend, Dalton. Dalton and I live in the same loft complex downtown where there was a triple homicide last year. Dalton teaches high school in Venice. Dalton, Milo is the editor of the arts section of the *L.A. Weekly*."

"Nice to meet you," said Milo, as the two diminutive gentlemen shook hands.

"Likewise," replied Dalton.

Another friend of Audrey's approached, a very smiley bespectacled girl, who gave her a warm hug.

"What about some drinks?" asked Audrey, turning to Dalton.

"Sure, what will it be?" he asked.

"I could go for a Vodka Cranberry," said Audrey. "But I'll get the drinks."

"No, no. It's on me," said Dalton, heading off to the bar as more friends clustered around her.

Standing at the bar amidst a small crowd having boisterous conversations and those eager to be served drinks, Dalton finally found a moment of relief from the claustrophobia of

Audrey's relentless networking. Finding an open bar stool, he plopped himself upon it.

"Whatever it is, don't sweat it. It will all blow over," offered the tall, curly-haired fellow sitting next to him.

Dalton didn't realize that his dismay was so evident.

"Really, it's nothing," explained Dalton. "My troubles are zilch. The girl that I'm hanging with this evening takes socializing to great extremes. She appears to have cultivated the acquaintance of every dolt in town."

"That really is nothing," said the tall fellow. "By the look on your face, I thought something heinous had befallen you."

"Well, thank you for being concerned," said Dalton, extending his arm to shake hands. "Dalton Everest's the name."

"Nathan Lyme."

"So what sort of pickles are you marinating, Nathan?"

"I'm not sure how to respond to that," said Nathan contemplating the odd, perspiring character with whom he had struck up a conversation. "I'm going to think about it and get back to you."

"This bar is like an old high school buddy whom I haven't seen in so long that I basically forgot he existed," said Dalton, "but he remembers absolutely every detail about me."

"I dig the crowd here," said Nathan. "You've got your typical alcoholics that you find in dive bars and then all these youngsters who have taken the place over. The oldsters are not ready to cede the place, but don't mind the half of the crowd that's young and female. The drinks are still cheap and the place still has character."

"Have you been to Bahooka?" inquired Dalton.

"Yes, the best tiki bar in town," said Nathan, "or really more of a nautical theme, kind of unique with such a focus on fish. I used to go to Kelbo's all the time on the Westside before the Northridge earthquake did it in. That was a neighborhood sort of Tiki bar, always fun. And Trader Vic's is still there, still schmanzy."

"Have you been to that tiki hotel in Palm Springs?"

"The Tropics, yes, I'm a sucker for any sort of postwar tiki kitsch," admitted Nathan.

"Old bars in L.A. are kind of fantastical, otherworldly," said Dalton.

"From the outside, it is often a not so beckoning wall of rocks with a little sign that says something like The Broom Closet or Smokey Timbers greeting would-be drinkers," said Nathan. "Then you open this door and you're in this barely lit, cave-like atmosphere. You have to wait until your eyes adjust to make out whatever unsavory characters are hanging out there, at a certain hour that is, say if it's some dive and you're arriving before happy hour. No matter how sunny it is outside, in L.A.'s drinking caves it's always night time."

"A Vodka cranberry and a martini, straight up," said Dalton finally getting his order in to the bartender.

"Ever heard of the Lowenbrau Keller?" asked Nathan.

"No, is that a Bavarian biergarten?"

"It's more of a kitsch Valhalla, a truly unique German restaurant stranded in a sketchy neighborhood west of Downtown. At night, there's nothing open around it for miles and the Lowenbrau also looks permanently closed. The owner was a prop designer and decked the place out in all manner of Teutonic wonderment: deer antlers, suits of armor, pseudo medieval tables and chairs, heaps of Germanic novelties. I've never seen him there, but his wife, Olga, a typically large German lady with a thick accent, runs the place by herself, handling the cooking, waiting tables, and dispensing high quality German beer, decent sausages and the like, too."

"I've got to check that place out," said Dalton, "sounds like a Nazi Disneyland."

"I usually go there on a week night, when it's completely dead. I've rarely ever seen another person there. If you want to go some time ..."

"Definitely!" exclaimed Dalton excitedly. "I know it's a little unusual to ask for a guy's phone number in a bar, but we're both into a lot of the same bull crap. You seem like some guy who has had his ass welded to a bar stool since the 1940s. I'm mad about the old Los Angeles and any remnants of it that are still lying around."

"Here's my number," said Nathan pulling a pen from his pocket and scribbling his number on a cocktail napkin.

Handing the napkin to Dalton, Nathan considered whether to also ask for Dalton's phone number on the off chance that Dalton never called him.

"What a ludicrous idea that is," thought Nathan. "I've met this little guy who has a crackerjack sense of humor and a peculiar way of putting things, but he's hardly a beautiful gal I want to bed. Why in the world would it mean anything to me if he doesn't call me?"

"Great," said Dalton collecting the drinks. "You will hear from me, Mr. Lyme."

Removing his lengthy inebriated frame from the bar stool, Nathan headed to the bathroom where he was not pleased to find himself peeing at a urinal with no piss protector between he and the next urinal. An old Black man in a black coat opened the bathroom door and grabbed the open spot that was too close to Nathan.

"Hanging low brother," the man said suddenly.

Puzzled, Nathan made eye contact with the man and saw from his face that he was clearly referring to Nathan's wanger.

"It's good to hang low," the man added, sloshed and smiling.

Not sure how to react to the compliment, Nathan zipped up his pants and sped out of there.

Meanwhile, in a booth near a popcorn machine that popped free popcorn for the Roost's patrons, Dalton spotted Audrey surrounded by her fan club.

"Where have you been?" she asked with a minor note of concern.

"I had a longish conversation with this guy at the bar," said Dalton.

After another hour of mingling, Dalton finally persuaded Audrey to head home. Originally, when Audrey, who lived one floor up from him, asked him out for the night, Dalton had been enthused. They'd hit it off on the elevator, especially when Dalton had mentioned that she looked like Cleopatra with a nose piercing, which she didn't. But now, as he drove them home, and she was the only one jabbering exclusively about what, he didn't know, Dalton found himself concentrating instead on the few moments he had spent talking with Nathan, almost as if the rest of the evening hadn't happened.

He pondered why Nathan had taken an obvious liking to him. Dalton couldn't think of anyone he knew who resembled Nathan. This mysterious and promising future pal was maybe two feet taller than him, handsome with the bone structure of an actor and remarkably cool in a way that Dalton found unfathomable. There was something a little bit shady about him that Dalton couldn't put his finger on. He sensed that Nathan might actually be a tough guy and perhaps sort of muscular, though it was hard to tell, as he was wearing a jacket. This got him wondering what Nathan might think of his friends if he were ever to meet them. They were not the hippest bunch, just a mixed-up variety of dorks, really. Dalton was probably a head cooler than all of them put together. There was also a certain confidence that Dalton had, even a cockiness that none of his friends possessed, which made him different from them, able to hold up a legitimate friendship with someone like Nathan, he believed. Dalton was proud that he had been in fights, lost some of them, sure, but won, at least one of them, though it had been maybe ten years previous. He was sure Nathan had been in a fistfight. It was a thrilling experience to be in an all-out brawl with someone. Dalton sometimes reminisced about the adrenalin-infused sensation of really mixing it up, which he believed he remembered accurately, but it was a memory with fear and pain conveniently edited out. He imagined himself and Nathan beating up skinheads together, though Nathan might actually be friends with skinheads, for all he knew.

As this fantasy became more idiotic by the second, Dalton realized Audrey was asking him a question.

"Don't we live on Spring? Why are we driving down Alameda toward the 10?" she wondered.

Three weeks later, Dalton was animatedly lecturing his class about Reconstruction, a period of U.S. history that he had studied, layering the subject with an abundance of detail that was mostly soaring over the heads of his students. Absorbed by his own oration and pursuing various tangents in every direction, he drew to a sudden halt when he noticed a hand raised at the back of the room.

"Yes, Cedric?"

"Um, ummm." There was a five second pause. "I was. I ... I ... forgot what I was gonna ask."

"Very well," replied Dalton resigned to the clear disconnect between his reverence for the material and his class's ho-hum attitude. "Does anyone else have any questions?"

Silence.

"We just have a few more minutes of class. I'm going to ask the few of you I haven't spoken with yet to come up individually to discuss your mid-term essays. Angelo, could you please come up?"

"Wus up?" said Angelo standing in front of Dalton's desk.

"Have you thought about what you might want to write about?"

"Naw. You know how it is Mr. Everest. I ain't got the time. I work after school. You know. I don't know if I can do it.

"You're failing this class," Dalton whispered. "Getting an essay to me is important. Usually, you show up here, you have that in your corner, but not much else. You have to give me something to let you squeak by with a C or D."

"Aw man, can't you just give me a C? I'm always here, listening, attentive. Honestly, I can't write papers."

"I don't care what the subject is, Angelo. You can write about Abraham Lincoln if you want. Just get me ten pages by Monday and we'll see what we can do, okay?"

"I'll try," said Angelo returning to his seat.

"Reina, can you come up?"

Reina, expressionless, slowly made her way to his desk, as if waging a silent protest.

"Have you written anything yet or chosen a subject?"

"I've taken some notes. I was going to write about Sherman's March to the Sea."

"Sounds great. Like it."

"However ... this weekend is my grandmother's 70th birthday and I'm going to be really busy. Do you think I could get an extension until next Friday? I would easily be able to finish by then."

Dalton was having a hard time imagining Reina, who had blonde hair with purple streaks and a lip piercing, spending the entire weekend celebrating her grandma's birthday.

"The due date is of course Monday, but if you can get me a well-researched paper by Friday, it'll work, I suppose."

"Oh, thank you, Mr. Everest. You're such a cool teacher."

The bell rang sonorously triggering most of Dalton's class to speed out of the room like greyhounds. A few of the girls, a group of friends who sat together, took their time collecting their piles of bags and books, as they discussed "a party at Deron's," which may or may not have been happening that weekend.

"They're not all muttonheads," reckoned Dalton. "One or two might amount to something or other. Craig will make his way to college, get laid there once or twice and eventually have a family and a very good-natured dog. Anita will perish a virgin, but before that will make a small fortune authoring a popular book about decorative artichoke displays or something. Carl, he has no chance in this world. He will likely be arrested for having sex with a dolphin, if that's illegal. And that will be the highlight of his existence, a story he will retell with that same ignoramus smile on his face for occasionally amused, but more often horrified strangers."

Upon receiving this post to teach at Venice High School, Dalton thought he was the luckiest duck in town. He had spent a brutal year at Crenshaw High School questioning if he had chosen the correct profession. At times, it had felt like a repeat of elementary school, where as a child, he had been relentlessly bullied. Waking up in the middle of the night, now as an adult, he would emerge from a nightmare, where a gang of mean kids had been chasing him down on dirt bikes, with him fleeing on foot, terrorized. A few of the worst kids at Crenshaw High, beyond not respecting his authority as their teacher in any fashion, had called him a twerp and made it clear that they could do physical harm to him without saying as much. As it had been in elementary school, Dalton feared mentioning the situation to his superiors, agonizing that he was somehow unfit for the job.

Scratching his chin while contemplating how his life had been rapidly improving, Dalton picked up his brown leather book bag and headed into the crowded school hallway. At Venice, the students were generally lethargic and unthreatening. Dalton's chief worry now was achieving the respect of the other teachers. Donning ugly corduroy sports coats and questionable striped sweaters, which he discovered were plentiful and cheap at the Goodwill in Burbank, Dalton had so far, in the eyes of some of his seasoned colleagues, only managed to look like a kid dressed up as a teacher.

As he entered the faculty parking lot, Dalton, brandishing the keys to his 1991 Honda Accord, which his parents had purchased for him before his undergraduate studies at San Francisco State, reveled for a moment in his validity as a member of the teaching class, something he had worked his ass off to achieve. Swinging his keys around dreamily and lording over his kingdom, Dalton swelled with pride at the exclusivity of the faculty parking lot and the fact that he possessed his own parking spot.

A short while after Dalton returned to his loft, his phone rang.

"Nathan, you wanton scoundrel!" Dalton shouted into the phone.

"Not really sure what to say to that," replied Nathan. "I was wondering what time you wanted to meet this evening."

"Um, how about 9?"

"Excellent. How about you and your chums meet me at the Formosa? Do you know where it is?"

"Yes and they are all very excited to meet you. I mean some of my friends are ... kind of ..."

"Squares or whatever, that's fine, you've warned me. I've met all sorts. Don't worry about it."

"I think maybe everyone will show up."

"Oh, a whole gang. Aces. See you then," signed off Nathan.

"He didn't waste any words," thought Dalton. "Maybe he was at work, though anything work related with him is Bermuda Triangle territory."

In the weeks since they had first met at the Roost, Nathan and Dalton had become inexplicably joined like beans and rice. They had soaked up the timeless Hollywood ambience of Musso & Frank, downing Musso's famous martinis, dining on steak and potatoes au gratin from a menu that hadn't changed much from the early part of the century and had there spotted local TV personality and California obsessive, Huell Howser. This sighting had spurred a debate between them as to the merits of Howser's homely documentary approach, which Dalton had called "expansive in its coverage of places you've driven by, wondered about, but not necessarily stopped for" to which Nathan had countered, "His show is barely edited and works the same as Ambien or horse tranquilizers."

A couple of nights later, Dalton had impressed Nathan with his discovery of an old-timey piano bar, recommended by Dalton's dad, Bob Henry's Round Table Restaurant in Santa Monica, where Nathan and Dalton, blitzed on cheap cocktails, had a spectacular bender. Nathan had spent an inordinate amount of time gabbing with the elderly waitresses, one of whom had told him her sullied life story. The fellow playing the piano, surrounded by a rounded piano bar table packed with sloshed regulars, was pretty good at hammering out a large canon of overly familiar music from Sinatra to Seventies easy listening. Late in the evening, Dalton found himself marveling at the pornographic wallpaper in the men's bathroom, for how long he did not know.

When the bar shut down at 2 am, they headed over to nearby Izzy's, an old Jewish deli open to the wee hours, for sobering borscht and rye toast. Still beyond the legal driving limit for alcohol intake, Nathan mentioned that there was a French girl, Melanee, whom he knew and would like to introduce to Dalton. He didn't elaborate much, but said he would talk to her. Dalton was intrigued, suspecting that Nathan knew people both distinguished and disreputable, though so far in their brief friendship Nathan strangely hadn't mentioned almost anyone he called friend.

And there it was, an unusual aspect of their budding rapport, which Dalton pondered and couldn't make heads or tails of. In his eyes, Nathan was sharp as a Ginsu knife, as handsome as David Beckham and as charming as anyone need be. He had witnessed girls, whom they had just met in bars, become googly-eyed over Nathan within seconds of him uttering a few sentences. Yet, Dalton, who had at first suspected Nathan was hiding his friends from him for the opposite reason that he had been hoping to conceal his own gaggle of high school pals, now wondered if Nathan was perhaps a loner of his own making. He hadn't mentioned if this French girl was a friend or an ex-girlfriend or what. This had been the first time Nathan had brought up Dalton meeting someone he knew and he had done so when he was clearly smashed and nearly slurring his words. As usual, when queried about the mysterious girl, Nathan had changed the subject. Dalton had never met anyone who was so cagey about such a vast amount of everyday bullshit.

So, that evening, in one of Hollywood's more storied watering holes, the Formosa, decked out in the faux Chinese exotica décor of yesteryear with Chinese lanterns and autographed head shots of Humphrey Bogart and the like, Dalton sat, apprehensively adjusting his eyeglasses, talking to his chief confidant, Leah, whom he had known since their seventh grade year at Arleta Junior High. It was in junior high, where Dalton's current group of friends had first met, Leah being the sole female member who still hung out with them occasionally. As close a friend as Dalton had, she had recently moved in with her longtime boyfriend and worked extended hours as a chef in a fancy Italian restaurant on Ventura Boulevard, causing her nonessential social life with former school pals to dwindle. Wedged way back in the distant past for both of them was the few months in which they had been a couple in high school. It was a frequent source of humor among the other members of the group, who joked about it when Dalton and Leah were not in earshot.

Though they had really clicked back in high school, it was Leah's cute but fundamentally nerdy looks, a bird's beak of a nose, thick eyeglasses, which truly reflected her learnedness, and a flimsy goose-like figure, which had given Dalton pause, turning their brief juvenile fling into a lasting and less burdensome comradeship. Relieved when Dalton broke up with her, Leah didn't care for Dalton's sporadically explosive temper.

"From your description he sounds like some sort of adult and perhaps like he might have it together, I mean compared to us," said Leah anticipating Nathan's arrival.

"He may have been a member of the cool kids and we clearly weren't," replied Dalton. "But there's this other thing about him that I can't quite figure. In the few weeks we've spent time together, I feel I almost look up to him in some ways and I'm sure that he finds me amusing and a fun person to get shit-faced with, but I don't feel like I really know him."

"What do you mean?" asked Leah.

"For instance, he mentioned that he's in post-production and I don't even really know what that is. But if I ask him any question about his work or where some drunken anecdote took place or who with or about high school or almost anything personal, he changes the subject in a slick way. Obviously, it's evident when he does it, but it's as if he's letting me know not to ask him about any of that stuff. It's unspoken, but pretty straightforward."

"Doesn't sound like anything to me. Dudley is in post-production. Why don't you ask him to ask Nathan about it? He'll know if that's really what he does for a living or if he's hiding something, but really, I doubt it. Why would he?"

Having carpooled, Dudley and Patrick, the other two members of the group, showed up a half hour late and joined them in a booth in what had once been a train car, which served as the back room of the Formosa. The two had been best buddies since ninth grade. Patrick, who was Japanese with family in California dating back to the turn of the century, had been the smartest of the bunch in school. He now worked for a successful internet related company doing something that none of them knew much about. More of an extrovert than the rest of the group and a veritable oddball, Dudley had a deeply held crush on Leah, which he had never revealed to the others, though he had on one occasion to Leah and had been roundly rejected.

Though Dalton wasn't too keen on the idea, Dudley eagerly agreed to talk post-production with Nathan. It was a subject he loved to gab about with anyone in the industry.

"Hey, nice to meet the gang!" declared Nathan materializing suddenly before them and smiling as he seldom did. "I told Dalton I was going to be late. Really wanted to make it here earlier, but had a busy day. Forgive me."

Wearing a snappy light blue suit without a tie and a striped fancy dress shirt, Nathan made an instant impression on all. The first round of drinks was on him and he asked about how they had all met, with interest. From the start, the evening went smashingly well and Dalton, after a few drinks, was envisioning Nathan fitting seamlessly into their tight group, though he was the only one thinking that.

While at the bar ordering another round and separated for a moment from the rest of the group, Dudley decided it was an opportune time to ask Nathan about his work.

"So, you are in post-production I hear?" he asked. "I am too. I'm working on an awful sitcom now from this idiot comedian who I'm sure you've never heard of, just one-liners and a laugh track. It's like family friendly hillbilly humor. What are you working on?"

Nathan's expression changed. It was a slight curling of the sides of his mouth downward. Dudley didn't notice.

"I'm between gigs right now. What would you like to drink, bub?"

"I'll get another Grolsch," answered Dudley. "What did you work on last?"

"It was a piece of junk too, something that won't even be released," replied Nathan.

"Whereabouts do you work? Are you somewhere in Hollywood?"

"Not working at the moment," replied Nathan. "Hey pal, I'm going to head to the other side of the bar right now and maybe the bartender spots me there."

Despite the brush off, Dudley followed him. He couldn't see any reason Nathan's employment history should be kept secret and supposed Nathan had worked on some big name show or film.

"You gotta tell me man. What stuff have you worked on?" Dudley persisted.

"Film, TV, some cartoons," replied Nathan now giving Dudley a stare down.

"Some titles?"

"Moron, Annoying Badgering Moron. Heard of it?"

"No," replied Dudley under his breath.

"That can't be the name of a show. Is he insulting me?" thought Dudley stunned.

"Are you ... what cartoons have you worked on?" he asked dejectedly and utterly baffled.

Nathan drew very close to him, grabbed his balls and gave them a little yank, clutching them, but not crushing them.

"I guess you don't need these," said Nathan. "If you want to lose them, keep asking me questions."

Dudley was speechless with fear.

"Look, I like Dalton a lot," explained Nathan. "He's a good guy. That doesn't mean I have to put up with your shit. When and if I release your balls, you're going to go back to the table and pretend nothing happened. You're going to say to your friends that I insisted on buying the drinks again. I'll bring them all over, don't worry about that. Do worry about asking me any further work related questions. You'll just act normal if you don't want me to rip these off."

Nathan tightened his grip.

"Got that?"

"Yeah," said Dudley, convinced.

Nathan glanced back at the table, which was obscured by a group of folks standing between them.

"Repeat it back to me," insisted Nathan.

"I'll go back. I'll act normal. You'll release my balls and buy the drinks," repeated Dudley.

What Dudley said about his balls sounded sarcastic to Nathan, though it wasn't. Nathan felt he hadn't driven home his point emphatically enough, so he squeezed.

Dudley turned white and pleaded.

"Please man, please."

The middle-aged, finely-coiffed man seated at a stool closest to them overheard and appeared to realize that something was amiss.

Nathan released Dudley.

"OK," Nathan whispered to him, "You go back there and do exactly what I said or you're horse meat."

Dudley sprinted back to the table.

While they were gone, Leah had spoken effusively about Nathan.

"He's gorgeous. I want to have sex with him."

"Good luck," said Patrick.

"You prick!" snapped Leah. "I didn't say I wanted to marry him."

Nathan returned twice to the table with everyone's drinks. He noted Dudley's downcast expression and felt his message had been received. He wasn't sure if Dudley was a troublemaker or just an imbecile. But he had no doubt that in assaulting him he had overreacted.

"So, did you all grow up in the Valley?" asked Nathan.

"I was born in Oakland," said Patrick. "We moved to Pacoima when I was eight."

"Pacoima," Dalton sighed. "Why hast the lord forsaken thee? I think we are all true Valleyites. We try and hide it, but deep down, we are not proud."

"North Hollywood is kind of happening now," said Patrick. "There's some effort on the part of someone to make it a center for the arts and such in the Valley."

"What about Glendale?" added Leah. "There is nothing wrong with Glendale. And La Cañada, La Crescenta, that area is mountainous and suburban, but attractive, not soul killing like Pacoima. Burbank has its moments, though I'm not really sure what they are. People of some distinction supposedly live in Toluca Lake or Sherman Oaks."

"Like who? Ricky Schroder from *Silver Spoons*?" said Dalton.

"Yeah, people like that I imagine, putting the San Fernando Valley on the map!" exclaimed Leah.

"The Valley's reputation as the butt crack of Los Angeles is entirely deserved," continued Dalton. "It's always been a hot bed of deranged professional weightlifters, porno hos from Utah and old men sitting and sweating in rickety plastic lawn chairs. To house all these suburban cuckoo birds, they built thousands of stucco apartment buildings and attached them to the shabbiest mini malls on Earth. That is the Valley I grew up in, a barren wasteland of debased humanity."

"It wasn't that bad," countered Dudley. "They used to have great punk shows at the Country Club in Reseda. I saw Fugazi, Bad Brains, and NOFX there."

"Yeah, and what about Busch Gardens?" argued Leah. "The theme park in Van Nuys where kids could go on rides while dad got plastered on free unlimited beer. My dad took me there every week during the summer. There was a monorail, one of those log jammer rides, and exotic birds, which are now wild and still roam the Valley. Growing up in Tujunga was groovy. It's like a thirty-minute drive over the hill to Hollywood from the East Valley. Wasn't like we grew up in Communist Albania."

Way before last call, Nathan bailed with no particular excuse for doing so, but with polite goodbyes to the whole group. Before leaving, he had mentioned to Dalton, while the others were chatting nostalgically about everyone they had hated in high school that he would be seeing the French girl, Melanee, the next day, and that he was sure she wanted to meet Dalton. This news was unexpected and threw Dalton for a loop, though it occurred to him soon after that he knew nothing about this girl, who Nathan had brought up twice with no details.

"Did you ever ask Nathan about his job?" Leah questioned Dudley after Nathan had departed.

"Oh man," replied Dudley. "Completely forgot about that. I guess next time."

"Annoying moron," continued to resound in Dudley's brain. He was still in shock and was not going to let the others know what had transpired and how he had done nothing to defend himself.

"Who was that jerk-off?" considered Dudley.

~ 3 ~

RANDOM STRANGERS

Dropping in on Melanee uninvited at three in the afternoon on a steamy day when Hollywood smelled like overheated asphalt, Nathan was conscious that he was going to utilize an unscrupulous method his dad had once employed. The idea being to successfully yank someone into a situation they might not wish to involve themselves in with just a little bit of the unexpected, a genuine or perceived threat and if required, a minuscule amount of violence. Melanee's pink apartment building, which Nathan had found for her six months previous, sat squat on the corner of Orange Drive and Fountain Avenue in crumbling disrepair. On the way there, driving down Sunset Boulevard, he had passed a guy in a tie-dye with spiky yellow hair and a Walkman dancing spastically at a bus stop like he was in a Prodigy music video and the image now made him chuckle.

Melanee answered the door wearing an oversized pajama top and blue panties, looking fetching, Nathan thought, considering his unplanned appearance.

"Do you have something for me?" asked Melanee by way of introduction. "I've been so bored."

"Your pony has come in, Sugar Bottom," replied Nathan grabbing her around the waist and pulling her toward him. "I have a job for you and it's painless. I just want you to get close with a pal of mine. He's an all-around, upstanding Joe. A real sweetie."

"I don't care if he is a little puppy," retorted Melanee, though with no effort to pull away from his firm embrace. "I am not a prostitute. Stripping is okay. If it is someone important, maybe a hand job. But nothing gross."

"It's not like that at all," explained Nathan. "I need you to be a sort of companion to him. Whether you sleep with him or not, doesn't matter. You're not to mention my business at all, how we met or anything that's happened between us. To him, you and I are strictly friends. But I want you to let him know that I'm responsible for you making his life sunnier, see? How you go about it, I don't care. It's three grand for the job, a grand now and the other two in a few weeks when I'm satisfied you two are cozy. Of course, he's not to know that you're being paid."

Melanee lit a cigarette offering one to Nathan, who declined.

"So, I don't have to sleep with him?"

"I'm not saying that exactly. If you want the other two grand, I need to be sure you're like two peas in a pod and that he knows I have done him a great courtesy. I don't care how you go about it. But it's important to me that you succeed. This gig's easier than the other jobs I've given you. In my mind, you're up to it."

"Why is it important that I get close to this man?"

"That's nothing you need to know."

"It's three thousand when he likes me?"

"That's the whole score."

"I was sure you would ask me to do another gross job like this," said Melanee, still disconcerted. "But I have my rent due yesterday. I'll do it."

"Of course you will. There was never any question of that. I wasn't asking you. You will do it and have a swell time of it," insisted Nathan, icily pulling ten hundred dollar bills from a clip and handing them to Melanee.

"I know you can be a lot of fun," continued Nathan. "I want you to be like a hay ride to my pal. There should be no reason for him to be interested in any other girl when you're on his arm."

"Who's the guy?" asked Melanee, placing the cash in a little tin box located in a kitchen cabinet.

"He's a school teacher. Can you beat that? A nice guy, handsome enough, funny, smart naturally, a shorty though, pint-sized really."

"I don't like little guys," said Melanee.

"And I don't care about your likes and dislikes," snapped Nathan.

"That's because you are a piece of shit."

"Where's your roommate?

"I haven't seen her. She hasn't been in for the last two nights. Why? You want to sleep with her? No problem. She sleeps with every drug addict who offers her a cigarette."

"I'll keep that in mind. I'll have my pal, Dalton, call you. I'll get his version of how things go, but you keep me updated too. That's all for now."

That afternoon, Nathan gave Dalton Melanee's phone number and mentioned again that she was eager to meet him. Dalton inquired why this French girl wanted to have anything to do with him. Nathan, vague as always, said he had mentioned Dalton a few times drawing interest from this lovely girl, who had only been in the country for eight months and needed to be shown around. Truly grateful, Dalton thanked Nathan profusely and said he would call her straight away. The only other time Dalton had been set up was by his mom, who had suggested he go out on a date with a friend's niece. That hadn't gone well. She had threatened to have him "beaten up" mid-date when he had casually touched her arm.

Breathing heavily with excited anxiousness, Dalton, wearing a tie and his favorite cream-colored dress shirt, rang Melanee's doorbell with no idea what lay before him. Over the phone, she had seemed shy and said almost nothing. An attractive blonde with long curls answered the door, but her voice lacked a French accent.

"Melanee will be ready eventually," said Allison, directing Dalton toward a futon, where he sat, discomfort swelling inside him. Allison leaned on a kitchenette counter staring at him with a puzzled look on her face.

"Water?" asked Dalton.

"Water?" replied Allison mean-spiritedly. "You want me to bring you water? You can get it yourself. There are a couple of clean glasses up there."

She motioned indifferently toward a cupboard.

Sweat running down his neck, Dalton grabbed a coffee mug and filled it with tap water, gulped it down, and poured himself another. Not wanting to return to the stained futon, Dalton stood next to Allison, who had not moved. Her scowl seemed to suggest a life-sized turd had suddenly appeared in her apartment guzzling tap water.

"Hello," said Melanee in a French accent that sounded to Dalton like an angel alighting from heaven.

"Hey, finally nice to be meeting you. I'm Dalton," he said scrambling his words.

"I know," said Melanee, picking up a silver purse and putting a key in it while differing from her roommate in avoiding eye contact.

Knowing not a thing about Melanee's appearance, Dalton was sold from his first glimpse. She was almost a head taller than him, dressed in a short blue skirt and pretty white, knitted shirt displaying curviness in all the right spots. She wore pink lipstick and was made up with a layer or two of powder and eyeliner. Her hair was fashionable, medium length, a hip, post-modern Euro cut with bangs at differing angles.

Dalton became, at once, aware that he had never gone out on a date with a girl remotely similar to Melanee. She was, to his eyes, both desirable and unattainable.

"Okay, you be good to her, weirdo," said Allison protectively. "I assume you're not a serial killer."

"Actually, I just dropped off a bag of mixed body parts in a dumpster on the way here," said Dalton recovering himself. "But not to worry, that girl was really slow in getting me a drink."

Opening the car door for Melanee with not a word spoken on the way to the car, Dalton asked, "Tell me about yourself, Melanee. Nathan, you know, didn't say anything. You're like Stonehenge, as far as I am concerned. What do you like to do?"

"Oh, I don't know," said Melanee licking her lips in a manner that was not sultry. "I want to know about you. Tell me what you like?"

"Anything exotic, Indian women with gold rings through their toenails or wombats are fantastic. Even something fake exotic is fine with me like the musical *South Pacific* or Peruvian guys playing flutes who suck at it. I like Béarnaise sauce. Smart people, as opposed to dumb asses. They're a dime a dozen and you just find them falling out of trees everywhere. I like tits. Usually, I stay away from the reefer, but once in a while … love Scotch or any kind of whiskey, Martinis. I guess I'm sort of a connoisseur of doughnuts, no Winchell's or Yum Yum for me. I will drive to Lomita for a quality doughnut, not playing about that. I like archery, but have never tried it. Someday. And I don't like yogurt, not at all, yuck."

"I don't like doughnuts. It's just a lot of grease, dough and sugar," commented Melanee.

"I'm sorry you feel that way," said Dalton smiling. "I will just pull over here and you can be on your merry way."

He pulled over to the curb.

"You're wacky," said Melanee laughing.

"That's the least of my charms," replied Dalton smiling like an animated horse.

Melanee was the third date that Dalton had taken to the Pacific Dining Car, close to Downtown. It was his go-to date spot, a wood-paneled, oftentimes deserted steakhouse, open at all hours with constantly hovering waiters and the refinement of yore. She didn't eat much and Dalton didn't notice. Loosening up quickly, Dalton was responsible for a large majority of the evening's conversation. He talked and Melanee listened, persuasively attentive. She was very much new to the town and country and Dalton liked that she seemed to not know much about anything. It was a long dinner and afterwards, Dalton wasn't sure where to take her, so he took her home.

"Give me a call. Let's hang out again soon," she said, and Dalton had goose bumps and a smile, now frozen where his usual less than cheerful face had once been.

The next day he called Nathan and heaped praise upon him, thanking him excessively. Impressed by how rapidly Dalton had been won over, Nathan dropped by Melanee's apartment, again uninvited, and handed her the second grand, adding that the third installment was hers as soon as he was confident that Dalton was hopelessly attached to her. Melanee was appreciative of the dough and Nathan sensed that she didn't mind the job so much. Something about his effective orchestration of their relationship made Nathan feel all-powerful, and with little resistance he had Melanee up against her kitchenette counter lanced and squeezing out rollicking orgasms.

For their second date, Dalton desired to sway Melanee to edge things onto a more romantic course. He took her to El Cholo, a Mexican restaurant on Western Avenue, which for decades had exuded an oddly comforting and familiar, typically gringo fantasy of Mexico. Sensationalizing the country as exotic and somewhat lawless, as it was to some degree, had been a popular theme in old Hollywood, while stateside Mexican restaurants chose to emphasize robust images of Mexican women in traditional dress preparing tortillas. With its enchilada sauce-colored tiles, adobe style architecture and nostalgia-covered walls, El Cholo encompassed in every way this ideal vision of Mexico. And Dalton, as an Angeleno, bought into that concept wholeheartedly, extolling every single dish to Melanee with sumptuous superlatives.

However, Mexican food was as foreign to Melanee as Captain Cook's arrival once was to native Tahitians. At Dalton's suggestion, she ordered the sweet green corn tamales, but consumed only a morsel. The fanciful décor seemed to make an impression, but as Dalton sang El Cholo's praises like he was playing a trumpet, it occurred to him that despite a somewhat obligatory smile that Melanee often wore, she was unmoved.

Aware that El Cholo hadn't worked any magic on her, Dalton next chose to take Melanee to a dive bar, the Smog Cutter, somewhat renowned for its karaoke, its surly Thai lady bartenders and well, that's it. No stranger to the Smog Cutter's dim spotlight, Dalton had himself listed as the evening's fourth performer and grabbed the mic confidently, picking one of his favorites, the theme song from the cartoon TV show, *Underdog*.

Dalton's rendition wasn't half bad and the tune was undeniably rousing. He could tell mid-song that Melanee was into it. He was possibly getting somewhere, or maybe not, it was hard for him to figure where he was at. Refusing to sing, Melanee was downing drinks like a storm gutter in a flash flood.

Away for a moment using the bathroom, Dalton was surprised upon his return to find Melanee talking to a buff, tattooed, mustached Mexican fellow wearing a tank top at the bar. For some reason, her hand was on his knee. Melanee introduced

Dalton and the guy quickly got the idea from Dalton's unsettled disposition that they were together and moved along. But the liquor in Melanee seemed to have done a number on her, causing her to laugh uncontrollably, to talk to random strangers in the bar, to get a little touchy with them and to blend in all too well. It was the most contented Dalton had seen her. He just wasn't sure if it had anything to do with him.

At closing, they got kicked out of the bar along with a sorry jumble of drunks, all seemingly now best friends with Melanee. She said goodbye to everyone, kissing them on both cheeks.

"Oh Dalton, you are not cute, but you are sweet like Red Hot Chili Peppers. I love the Red Hot Chili Peppers," declared Melanee, as Dalton idled his car in front of her apartment building.

"That music is utter pig manure," replied Dalton.

"No," Melanee cried. "It is goooood."

He was then flabbergasted when she leaned over, whiskey-breathed, and kissed him hard on the lips. The act was as indelicate as a wet smack on the mouth. But Dalton recovered, slid his fingers through her hair and kissed her back. The whole experience was kind of rough and unsettling, in no way how Dalton had imagined it might be.

"But you are so petit, eh, and small," she said drawing away from him in drunken contemplation. "Why couldn't you be a little bigger?"

"You are like up to my tits. I have to bend down," she continued snickering to herself. "Why don't you grow a little bit?"

Dalton turned beet red; his mortification quickly swelling into raw fury. It had been a long time since anyone had ridiculed him like that.

"You need to get out of my car, you two-bit, frog-chewing tramp," he said unsteadily.

"Two bit" and "frog chewing" meant nothing to Melanee, but "get out of my car" registered horror and bewilder-
ment upon her. In her trashed state, she realized that she had
erred grievously.

"No," she said trying to square things, "I didn't mean
that. You are very handsome and funny. That's why I kiss you. I
didn't know what I said."

She grabbed him by the collar and kissed him the same
way only harder with more of a thrust of her tongue. After some
half-assed resistance from Dalton, he succumbed. He wanted
her bad. And the insults melted away.

After a minute or so more of sloppy drunk smooching
from Melanee, met with wholesome, conservative, semi-heart-
felt kissing from Dalton, Melanee again abruptly drew away.

"I'm sorry what I said. You know I am sorry. You call
me."

She stumbled out of the car.

~ 4 ~

LA VIE EN ROSE

Opening her eyes the following afternoon, Melanee at first recalled a night spent clutching the toilet seat with fits of sleep in between and occasional feigned concern from Allison. Sitting up on the living room futon, Melanee lit a cigarette. With a regular job at a nail salon, Allison paid the majority of the rent for the apartment and occupied the only bedroom. Melanee essentially sublet the futon in the middle of the living room, the closet next to the bedroom, and various spots around the apartment where she stored her few belongings. Growing up in Nice, France, she had shared her bedroom with two older brothers, so privacy had always been an alien concept.

She had no energy to make coffee and there was none anyway. Gulping a glass of tap water, she walked in circles around the futon, aching. After some thought, it came back to her that she had insulted Dalton the night before, said something about his height, and he had been deeply offended. Not sure how things had been left, she realized she needed to call him.

"Dalton, I'm sorry I was a horrible bitch last night," she told his voicemail. "Remember, I am nice sometimes. Forgive me, I was drinking like an idiot and said some brainless things, which I didn't mean. Of course, I really like you. Please call me when you get back from school, okay?"

Content with the message she'd left and certain that Dalton would call her as soon as he could, Melanee decided she would shower, throw something on, and spend the day wandering around Hollywood, her chief daytime occupation. Dependent on rides from Allison, Nathan, and a few other friends and admirers to get anywhere distant in town, while not yet bothering to figure out the bus system, Melanee spent a lot of her time hoofing it across Hollywood, wearing down the heels of her black boots. Her two favorite streets for exploration were the past-its-prime Melrose, and raggedy, cat-piss-smelling Hollywood Boulevard. Feeling like she had been in a boxing match the night before, Melanee figured she wasn't up for the hike to Melrose and back, so chose the shorter distance to Hollywood Boulevard.

Stomping heavily up Highland Avenue, Melanee passed the fellow she called The Garbage Bag Man sitting at one of his usual spots in front of a chain-link fence, wrapped in a black garbage bag. He had long, matted brown hair and appeared twenty years older than his actual age.

"Pretty whore, let's grab a bottle and have good times," he mumbled in a hoarse voice in Melanee's general direction.

She didn't catch the words, smiled and walked on.

Further down the road, she passed a guy with a broken lip and then a group of Latino kids on bikes who gave her the once-over. The constant staring and comments didn't faze her. It had been worse in France, where the most lurid things had been spouted at her from strangers. Melanee actually thought herself somewhat fortunate in that she believed many girls who looked plain or average were universally ignored by passers-by.

Arriving at the McDonald's on Hollywood Boulevard, Melanee spotted some familiar faces out front amongst the cluster of gutter punks who regularly panhandled there.

"Melanee, where you been?" greeted Sam, a chubby 16-year-old with red cheeks, short dyed orange hair, and a beat-up leather jacket with cut-off sleeves, "I got some meth. I thought maybe you'd want to buy some more."

"No, my roommate is broke. She can't afford it right now. She's the one into that stuff," said Melanee. "Maybe some other time. Got a smoke?"

"Naw, you got a smoke, Gunny?" he asked the oafy, freckled kid next to him.

"Yeah," he said, handing Melanee a cigarette and a lighter.

Melanee had a couple of loose cigarettes and at least three lighters in her purse.

"Thanks," she said.

"Melanee's French," Sam told Gunny.

"Do you know Gérard?" Gunny asked Melanee.

"Who's Gérard?" she replied.

"You don't know Gérard?" asked Gunny in the sluggish, lunkheaded voice that complemented his considerable size. "He's French. He was squatting on Las Palmas up until recently. He's in jail now or deported, I don't know. He got into mugging tourists, even though he was a fuckin' tourist. I don't know where he got the idea. I think he made some dough for a short while. But then he got in a tangle with this Black lady, who beat the shit out of him. She smashed his head against a newspaper box and was dragging him by his foot along Hollywood Boulevard. He was a skinny guy and no match for this lady. Squirt saw the whole thing. He was trying to intervene and ask this lady to let go of Gérard. The police finally showed up and Squirt ran off. We haven't heard anything about Gérard since. He owes me a bag of pot."

Melanee considered that she would have liked to have met Gérard. She had encountered only a couple of French people in L.A. and longed to speak French with anyone. She noticed

Juan, who gave her a nod, and Ernesto standing nearby talking to some puny girls. Juan and Ernesto had a band called Fetid Scum, who were somewhat renowned in the tiny underage punk scene in Hollywood. They lived several blocks away in an apartment with their parents.

Sometimes, Melanee would spend an hour or two in front of the Hollywood Boulevard McDonald's shooting the shit. But on this day, rather than aimless wandering and chattering with nincompoops, she had come up with an objective, shoplifting some new lingerie. Shoplifting was one of Melanee's favorite hobbies (though it had sometimes been key to her survival) and she had found it to be remarkably effortless in Los Angeles. There always seemed to be someone young and inattentive working in the stores.

Traipsing through the scum of Hollywood Boulevard on a sunny afternoon, Melanee passed a vacationing family in matching bright orange church T-shirts, stores dedicated to junk emblazoned with images of Marilyn Monroe and Elvis, two fellows having a loud, misogynistic conversation about what women want, and the police rousting some Latino teenagers in a souped-up hot rod.

Opening the door to Fredrick's of Hollywood, Melanee was greeted by the pink-haired, freckled girl with the nose-piercing, whom she recognized from when she dropped in a couple of days before. Quickly surmising that conditions were advantageous for shoplifting with no other customers or people in the store, Melanee went at it the moment the girl turned in the opposite direction. She grabbed the chemise and baby doll she had picked out the other day and quickly shoved them into the back of her jeans. Melanee then set about looking like a normal customer. She picked out $4 panties, purchased them and walked out of the store. It had been a cinch. A couple of blocks away, she stepped down a side street, pulled the lingerie out of her jeans and placed it in her purse.

Now aglow with the satisfaction of pulling it off so easily, Melanee felt fully recovered from her hangover and skipped down Cahuenga Boulevard. Passing a glammy looking rocker dude in a leather jacket, she stopped, thinking he looked familiar.

"Were you in L.A. Guns?" Melanee asked.

"No, I loved that band. I get that sometimes. I was in a whole bunch of groups, though" the man replied warmly.

"Which ones?"

"Oh, gee, I am in a Deep Purple cover band now called Perfect Strangers. I played drums for Trick Nixon, Lady Snake, and in the Eighties, I played with the Dastardly Rascals, though if you are familiar with them, I should probably keep that to myself," he said chuckling.

"Hey, nice to meet ya. I'm Jake," he added shaking hands with her.

"Melanee."

"Where are you from?"

"France."

"Cool! Wow! France. How long you been here?"

"Almost a year."

"Oh, a real newcomer. I'm from Idaho, but have lived in L.A. for twelve years, except for a short spell in Dayton, Ohio with my brother, while I was rehabbing. Don't ever want to go back there. I was just heading to my pad. You want to smoke some bud?"

"Why not," said Melanee.

Jake lived on the third floor of an apartment building two blocks north of Hollywood Boulevard on Cahuenga. It was a small studio apartment heaped with layers of rock & roll paraphernalia covering all surfaces: broken cymbals, empty cigarette packs, loose CDs, Modern Drummer magazines opened at a particular page (there were four of them in different spots around Jake's living room), pizza boxes, a water bong, drumsticks, bandanas, empty beer bottles, cheap jewelry, ticket stubs, as well as two scattered drum sets.

Taking it all in, Melanee thought the place was magnificent.

"My cleaning lady doesn't get around very often," said Jake sarcastically.

"Your apartment is amazing," gushed Melanee. "I have always wanted to live in a place like this. My roommate is so uptight. You are a rock & roll guy who likes to have a good time and so your apartment is like that. It's genuine."

"Thanks," said Jake, "I've never received any compliments before about this dump. What kind of music do you dig?"

"I like all of it," replied Melanee, "but I am crazy for hair metal, that whole pretty boy scene, dressing up in furry boots and bright colored Spandex, looking hot and living fast, drinking whiskey from the bottle and every part of the hard rock lifestyle. I would have loved to have been there on the Sunset Strip in the Eighties and seen Dokken, Pretty Boy Floyd, Guns N' Roses, Faster Pussycat, Kix, and Bon Jovi. I have all of their cassettes with me, but I don't have a player now, so I haven't listened to any of them since I was back home."

"It was incredible to be here when all that was going on," recalled Jake. "I used to hang out at the Cathouse every week and everybody was there. I remember one time in the bathroom I bumped into that dude from Poison snorting cocaine with a bunch of skanks. I thought one of the bands I was playing with might get somewhere because a lot of the bands were getting signed to majors, never happened. But it was a heckuva fun time while it lasted."

"I am so jealous."

"I work at Guitar Center now. A lot of the guys from the bands you mentioned come into the store."

"That's incredible," replied Melanee, still effusive.

"So, how did it come about that you came to Los Angeles?"

"I will tell you, but it's a messed-up story."

Soon after her arrival in Los Angeles, Melanee had desired to open up to somebody about her precarious existence and how things had gone sour in her life practically from the outset. But she had ruled out Dalton or Allison since they were both a little too close to her present situation. Jake seemed like a very decent guy to Melanee and he was entirely removed from the few other people she knew.

"I grew up in a slum in the south of France," she recounted." My father played cards all the time and lost, and my mom was always upset and had no money. She would go out searching for my dad in the middle of the night and sometimes returned the next morning but without him. Most of the time, my two brothers and I were left on our own. We had nothing, basically. When I was twelve, my brother Anton introduced me to some thieves who taught me how to pickpocket. They kept everything I stole, every penny. Later, they taught me how to grab purses. I became very good and they had to pay me a little money for all I did. I could spot a designer purse from two blocks away. I still can, but I don't try it here because I don't know how to sell them. I was never involved in that part of it. I would go to a fancy neighborhood in Nice, spot a smaller or older lady by herself with an expensive bag. I knew all the brands, Gucci, Prada, Chanel, Louis Vuitton. I'd ask them for change and then when they were looking for some coins, I would just grab their purse away and run, and I was fast, super fast. They never caught up with me. Well, two times, yes, but I just gave them back their bags and kept running. Of course, these guys I worked for were always trying to get me to sell my body for sex and a few times when I was desperate and drunk, I went along with it."

"Really!" said Jake, mouth agape.

"Yeah. Let me tell you. It was terrible. I did get some real money out of it, though. Then one day, I met this American guy, Nathan, who I really liked. He took me out to dinner. I thought I was his girlfriend. I asked if I could come to America with him. We flew to Los Angeles. I just grabbed my stuff and didn't get a chance to say goodbye to my family, though I didn't really care to. I wanted to be rid of them, forever. At the same time, I mean, I had a feeling that wherever I was going might be bad. But I didn't really care because where I was coming from was a piece of shit. When we got to Los Angeles, Nathan stopped treating me like I was his girlfriend. He tried to make me do various criminal jobs. We robbed a house. He said I was no good at that. He said I knew designer handbags, but I could never understand the value of anything else. He said I was naturally loud and dumb and he could never depend on me, and I was just going to get him arrested. But he did find me my apartment. He got me some modeling jobs, I guess, if you want to call them that. Now, he has me hanging out with this nice guy. They are friends, I guess. But this other guy, he's very normal and strangely kind to me, a schoolteacher, but funny. I mean I don't like him that way. But I don't mind going out with him."

"I'm just curious. I don't mean to be prying, but is he paying you to have sex with this guy?"

"Probably he is, though I haven't yet. But Nathan is an odd guy. I've given up trying to figure him out. He's a bad person and basically all I have here. I've overstayed my visa. I don't think I can legally get a job and I've never had a normal job in my life. I don't know if I could stand the boredom. I'm kind of stuck. I mean I'm not asking anything from you. You just seem like a nice guy I can talk to about this sort of shit."

"This guy, Nathan, he's not going to come over here and harm me because you're here at my apartment, is he?" asked Jake nervously.

"No, he doesn't know I'm here and he wouldn't care anyways. He doesn't control me."

"You're sure? Because I don't have much money or anything. Maybe I'm not the best client."

"I just said you seemed like a nice guy I could talk to. I didn't think of you as being a client. I don't have clients," replied Melanee raising her voice defensively.

"I mean, thanks for saying I'm nice. But isn't this other guy sort of a client? The guy you mentioned that you are supposed to have sex with or hang out with or whatever. That doesn't sound like an ordinary relationship. I don't want to have any part of any sort of criminal activity. I'm from Idaho. I like to party, have a good time, but I don't believe in paying to have sex with someone or especially stealing from old ladies. I just wasn't brought up that way, know what I mean?"

Melanee was speechless.

"Maybe we could get stoned some other time, if that's okay," he added.

"Thank you, I'll leave," answered Melanee, her face twitching.

She rushed out of the apartment, slammed the door, though not purposely, and rushed down the stairs and then outside. As she crossed Yucca Street, she started blubbering uncontrollably.

"Ma'am, are you okay?" asked a scruffy youth in a Polo shirt crossing the street.

"Fuck you!" Melanee roared and ran frantically back to her apartment.

That night, Dalton had plans to meet up with Nathan at one of the oldest bars in Los Angeles, Cole's, which was situated in the middle of skid row downtown, not far from Dalton's loft. Loopy over Melanee, Dalton had forgiven her even before receiving her apologetic message. The instant he returned home, Dalton listened to Melanee's voice on his answering machine, grabbed the phone and asked Melanee if he could pick her up that night. His plans for all three of them to hang out together struck Melanee as something best avoided.

"I have to cut back on drinking," she said. "I don't feel comfortable in bars. And I found out this guy I know, Gérard, died today. He was the only French person I knew in Los Angeles."

"That's awful," said Dalton. "I'm sorry to hear that. What happened to him?"

"I don't know really. No one told me the story. I'd like to go out, but it's really just not a good night."

"I want to see you," said Dalton dramatically. "Last night didn't go that well and I would like to make up for it."

"But I was the one who was evil and you were basically a gentleman."

"Come on out with me."

"Fine."

Just after the call, Melanee rang Nathan, who didn't sound nervous about the evening, but decided to swing by Melanee's anyways. He walked up the steps just as Allison was returning home.

"Hey there kiddo," he said to Allison.

"What decade are you from?" she asked.

"A better time, no doubt, when men wore pants and ladies smoked long cigarettes."

"I think I have asked you before, but what do you do for a living?"

"I do everything. You name it."

"That's vague. Are you a notorious international criminal?"

"Yes, that too. Were I, would that interest you?" asked Nathan.

"You're plenty cute. But I don't think my roommate would go for us spending time together. I'm pretty sure she is hung up on you. I try and be a good girl, though I fail at it most of the time."

They entered the apartment and found Melanee sitting on the sofa watching *Friends* on TV. In a T-shirt and panties with some eye shadow on her cheek from when she had been crying earlier, Melanee looked ravishing to both Nathan and Allison.

"Hey there, Sugar Bottom," said Nathan.

"Ah, don't call me that, you asshole," she replied perturbed.

"Now, now. How about you get up, put something on and we'll go out for a coffee?" said Nathan.

"Fuck you. I'm watching this," said Melanee motioning to Lisa Kudrow on the TV screen.

"I'll leave you two lovers to each other," said Allison heading to the bathroom.

"Get the fuck up," said Nathan to Melanee as soon as Allison was out of earshot, "and put something on."

Melanee dressed and primped herself as leisurely as any woman could and they drove over to the nearby coffeehouse, Uncommon Grounds.

"I'm sorry," said Melanee. "I had a shitty day."

"What happened?" asked Nathan.

"I found out the only French guy I know in L.A. died."

"Sorry, that's too bad. What happened to him?"

"I don't have the whole story."

"So, tonight, Dalton is sure to ask about how we met. You haven't mentioned anything to him about that of course, have you?"

"No, I didn't mention that."

"Good. We'll say we met here in L.A. We met at a bar, Bar Deluxe on Las Palmas. We became friends, that's it."

"I've been to Bar Deluxe."

"Swell. That's where we met. And how are things going with Dalton?"

"OK I guess. How long do I have to hang out with him?"

"It's open ended. If you were to break it off with him, that would really spoil things. There will be more money in it for you down the line, if you keep smiling and play the happy girlfriend."

"How much money? I'm still owed a thousand."

"We'll see how things go tonight."

"I don't mind him at all. I wish he wasn't always trying to impress me with his knowledge of everything and his big words. But he's a very decent guy, say, compared to you."

"He is a decent guy," said Nathan. "He's probably my closest friend. We have had some great times together. Despite what he has told me, I don't think he has scored much with the ladies in this lifetime. Now, Sugar Bottom, let me tell you, you are one sexy box of Godiva chocolates. You are a Class A babe and I'm sure Dalton is thanking his lucky stars."

Melanee smiled at the unexpected compliment.

"I am doing him a real favor," continued Nathan. "But I don't want him to know that you and I ever had any kind of relationship, which wasn't paly-waly."

"Got it," said Melanee, changing her expression.

Later, Dalton, feeling nearly overcome by his romantic fantasies, arrived at Melanee's and kissed her quickly on the mouth with an ounce or so of self-confidence. The puppy-like expression on his face made Melanee's stomach turn. She had no tolerance for any sort of sap. It always grossed her out when someone put their arm around her or said something tender to her that reminded her of Julio Iglesias.

At Cole's, an old-timey, saloon-looking bar that oozed character and history and appeared much as it had when it opened near the turn of the century, Dalton and Melanee were met by Nathan and a blonde, Clara, who greeted them with a

Boston accent, which sounded like she was smacking them in the face with a fish. Overly tan, curvy, young and obtuse as a stick of gum, Clara was to Cole's and its seedy habituates what a twirling hippy girl is to a Grateful Dead concert. Nathan had met her just a couple of nights before at Frank N Hanks, a Koreatown dive that remained off the hipster radar. He had picked her up with ease, but was already questioning his decision to bring her along for the evening after she had sneezed, splattering snot on the dashboard of his Audi.

"This drink tastes like Lysol," said Clara after they had ordered and were seated somewhat uncomfortably at a low wood table.

"You want some of mine?" asked Dalton, offering her his martini.

"No thanks, I'll just spill that," said Clara.

"When I was in college I could drink like a whale," said Dalton, "and now, I feel like it hits me a little harder than it should. Three drinks is pretty much my limit."

"Where did you go to college?" asked Clara.

"Stanford," replied Dalton, "San Francisco State for my Bachelor's."

Everyone was impressed, though keeping it to themselves. No one else at the table had attended college at all.

"At San Francisco State, I took a French lit class. I was nuts about Zola. Are you into Zola?" Dalton asked Melanee.

"Who's Zola?" she asked.

"You've never heard of Zola, the French novelist?" replied Dalton in disbelief. "He wrote the Rougon-Macquart series of 20 novels of which *La Bête humaine* is perhaps the most exceptional. It's fundamentally a crime novel. Hollywood made it into a film noir called *Human Desire* directed by Fritz Lang and there's also an earlier French version with Jean Gabin."

No one had much to add to Dalton's burst of literariness.

"What about Stendhal? You read Stendhal in school?" he asked Melanee.

"I mostly, what do you call it, didn't go ... "

"Ditched," suggested Nathan.

It began to occur to Dalton that his questions were making Melanee appear unschooled. He had at first been dumbfounded that she had never heard of Zola, but now he noticed the flustered look on her face. Melanee quickly took to downing drinks. Both she and Clara tore through cocktails like bulls at Pamplona, while Nathan and Dalton were dawdling, contemplative drinkers.

"Are you two together, I can't tell?" Clara asked Dalton and Melanee.

"No," said Melanee dismissively at the very same moment Dalton whispered, "yes."

Revived from her stupor, Melanee put her arm around Dalton and hiccupped, "It doesn't matter."

But the train of thought Melanee had had before the question egged her forward.

"What I was wondering is, are you two fucking?" she asked Clara.

Nathan tried to hold back his glare, but did not succeed.

"I let him play with my tits some, but no, we just met," Clara answered bawdily.

"Both boobs, or just the left one?" asked Dalton.

"Both," replied Clara.

"Forgive me, I'm out of it," said Melanee. "Again, I've gotten myself drunk and I guess it was a long day and I'm feeling kinda sleepy."

"You're not on heroin, are you sweetie?" asked Clara.

"I wish I was. I'm sure heroin would be incredible. No, I'm just a bit drowsy," replied Melanee.

"How exactly would heroin be incredible?" asked Dalton aghast. "What is romantic at all about a drug that sucks the soul out of its victims and leaves them as ice cold slabs of grayish meat?"

"What a way to go, though," added Melanee. "I'm sure it would be a fantastique way to leave this world. I must try heroin. Got any heroin, Nathan?"

"I've got some Life Savers in my back pocket."

An evening that had so far been like batting around a baseball in a closet deteriorated precipitously when Melanee gravitated toward the bar area and struck up a conversation with a man wearing a flannel suit. Within minutes, her arm was around his shoulder and his arm was at her waist with his hand at the top of her butt crack. They appeared to be having an animated conversation. Nathan was not keen on Melanee's behavior, but he could not conjure up an idea of how to take control of the situation. As Dalton sunk into his seat in deep dismay, Melanee's elbow knocked a glass off the bar and it somehow soared toward the middle of the room, banking off the side of a table, where a sad, destitute man was sitting practically unaware of his surroundings, and then crashed on the floor, turning the eye of everyone in the now crowded room. Without saying anything, Dalton immediately ran out the door.

"Let's get out of here too," Nathan said to Clara, though he was baffled at Dalton's sudden reaction.

Nathan picked up Melanee from her bar stool, dropped a wad of cash on the bar and apologized to the bartender. Melanee gave a little protest and Nathan bent her thumb back, eliciting a scream. Now all fifteen or so people in the room were staring at them. Detesting all scrutiny, Nathan, with uncustomary redness in the face, shoved Melanee out the door.

Outside on the cold, empty street, Nathan whispered to her, as Clara chased after them. "I don't know what happened to Dalton. He ran out the door when you broke that glass. You need to patch things up with him quick like, if you ever want to see another dime from me."

Melanee's survival skills were strong, even in her current diminished state.

"Where is he? I'll handle it," she slurred.

The three of them walked down the block and turned on South Main Street, passing a couple of mariachis wearing sombreros and carrying guitar cases. Melanee had no idea where Dalton had parked. They then backtracked in the other direction and were starting to consider the possibility that Dalton had taken off, when Nathan spotted his silver Honda Accord parked near the corner of South Los Angeles Street and East 6th Street, with Dalton inside.

Melanee went around to the driver's side and Dalton rolled down his window.

"I'm sorry," she said, and tried to kiss him through the window bumping her head on the roof of the car. Dalton pushed her back in a childlike manner, seeming to be on the verge of tears.

"Can you give her a ride home?" he yelped at Nathan.

"No, you give her a ride home," said Nathan. "She's a good kid. She just gets ripped more easily then some. Forgive, forget, whatever."

"OK," said Dalton in easy defeat, and Melanee got in on the passenger's side.

They were silent as they drove back to Melanee's apartment, she wishing that she were soberer, distressed that she might lose Dalton and perhaps her only current, tangible way of making a buck.

"I'm sorry again," said Melanee nervously. "I think maybe I love you and want to run away with you somewhere."

The running away part was at least sincere to a point, though not in any way thought out.

"What?" replied Dalton in astonishment.

"I think you are a really good person," she went on. "I know, maybe we are not exactly alike. But you are giving and kind and that is rare. Los Angeles is filled with assholes. I'm not like that and you're not like that. Let's get out of here and go somewhere simpler, some place where people eat eggs and pancakes for breakfast and read the newspaper and breathe better. I'd love to breathe real air again that didn't contain so much nastiness. There's got to be a place like that and it's probably not even far away. Let's get out of this shitty hole in the ground and speed off somewhere tonight! What do you say?"

"I'm humbled and flabbergasted I guess," began Dalton trying to rein in all his conflicting thoughts. "I love you too. You are a vision. The drinking, though, doesn't seem to agree with you. I can't just run off tonight. I have a job that I enjoy. Those kids depend on me showing up every day, or at least I like to fantasize that at least a couple of them give a damn. L.A., it's not the most fresh-faced town, but it invariably charms the bejesus out of me without even trying. Diners abound with decent pancakes. If I was forced to leave here, I would do so with you on my arm, but I have both feet planted firmly."

"Oh, okay, you suck, sorry I asked," replied Melanee, offended and now lost in her own cloud of despair.

"You know, you're like a Roman candle with both ends lit," said Dalton.

"Maybe we could go shopping together some time instead," said Melanee. "You really need to get some decent clothes. That plaid shirt looks like its fighting with that, what do you call it, corduroy jacket."

When they arrived at her apartment, Melanee, still cock-eyed and somewhat sick to her stomach, could not force herself to kiss Dalton and was relieved when he made no such move either.

"Give me a call," said Melanee. "I meant everything I said about you being a good guy. Let's go out soon, though maybe somewhere without drinks."

"I will wire you a telegram shortly," replied Dalton.

"Yeah," slurred Melanee.

That evening, utterly mystified by what had befallen him, Dalton called his trusted friend, Leah.

"What the hell do you want, blockhead? It's eleven. I have curlers in my hair and a boyfriend who nods off the second the Lakers highlights are over."

"Sorry. Really? Curlers? That would be a sight. I used to call you late and you didn't complain."

"I was single and living at my mom's house with my own phone line. Now, I'm an adult with a life. What's wrong with you? Your voice is all parakeet like. Did that tart you're going out with break your heart? If so, not surprised."

"She said she wants to run away with me," explained Dalton. "And while relating this, in a sort of roundabout way, she interposed that she might be in love with me. Though, it's all been up and down and back and forth like a tennis game on acid. But I've fallen for her hard. It's as if the floor has given out. There's just her. Everything else is in the background."

"Don't run away with that tart, Dalton!"

"Actually, I would appreciate it if you didn't call her a tart."

"What is her name?"

"Melanee."

"This girl is mixed-up. She can't handle her liquor. She is a Frenchy and may have other boyfriends for all you know. Clearly, she doesn't know what the hell she wants. She is like a newspaper with a huge, bold headline warning you of impending danger. But you're just nonchalantly reading the story and soaking up all the details without concentrating on the headline. What do you know about her anyways?"

"Really, not much. She is not as cagey as Nathan, but not forthcoming in any way. Once she mentioned she doesn't have any contact with her family, so I have not broached that subject.

She seems to regard the town from which she came in France, I forget the name, with equal disdain to here. I get the idea that she has a lot of free time. Whenever we are in a bar with an especially inebriated group of bums, she gravitates to them and mixes in like they're all long lost cousins of hers. I turn my head and some guy will have his hands all over her. I've wondered if she is a stripper."

"Dalton, if you could listen to yourself on my end of the line, you would clearly hear a person sinking with giant rocks strapped to his wanger. You are a good person. You need to get out of this predicament while you still can."

"I don't see it as a bad thing that Melanee has feelings for me too. I've been like a candy-thieving child since I met her."

"I don't know what that means. That doesn't mean anything. I have to get up at 6:30 tomorrow to go to the farmer's market. Keep me abreast of your downfall."

"Okay, see you on the downswing. Thanks."

"I don't know what that means either. I'm sure that doesn't mean anything."

~ 5 ~

A VERY DECENT GUY

It was a crisp Saturday morning, the air extravagantly moist, the sun beaming down, steadily warming all. With a lift to his step, Dalton went to procure coffee at the dumpy little place he often frequented near his loft, but was dismayed to find that it was now closed on Saturdays. There was a man slumbering below the window out front, wrapped in a ripped sleeping bag. An impetuous mood suddenly seized him and upon returning home he called Melanee, waking her from a nightmare, wherein she had been seized and strangled by a sweaty man wearing a white paper mask and breathing heavily. She agreed to go on a hike in the hills with him, though after putting the receiver down immediately regretted that decision.

When Dalton arrived at her apartment, she was in the shower, still preoccupied with her paper-masked strangler. Knocking vigorously, Dalton heard the distant sound of running water and stood there impatiently for a half hour or so. He knocked again, thinking the shower sound had gone away, but it returned. Now starting to lose it, he pounded on the door and Melanee arrived, wrapped in a brown towel, apologized and traipsed quickly back to the bathroom. Ensconced for an eternity in the messy living room, Dalton still retained the jovial, somewhat daring mood from earlier in the morning and was resolute that he and Melanee would turn over a new leaf.

"You're sure you want to go on a hike?" asked Melanee emerging in cut-off shorts, her big black boots, and a tight red shirt that read "Poison" on the front.

"The weather is perfect and the hills are gorgeous around here. Have you ever been?

"I don't much care for nature."

Undaunted, Dalton drove them through Los Feliz and made a left on Crystal Springs Drive at the entrance of Griffith Park, the mountainous city park that bisects Los Angeles at the eastern section of the Santa Monica Mountains. Proceeding past the pony rides and the kiddie railroad, he made another left into the large parking lot near the time-machine-like Griffith Park Merry Go Round and its blaring Stinson military band pipe organ.

They exited his car and walked south, Melanee following Dalton listlessly, and proceeded past a road barricade and then made a left at the trailhead for Fern Canyon Nature Trail and then another left.

"That trail heads to the old zoo picnic area," said Dalton pointing to a dirt road. "You can hang out in the rusty cages and dine on raw meat."

"That sounds like a good time. Let's check it out," replied Melanee perking up a bit.

"Maybe we should catch it on the way back," suggested Dalton. "It would probably be a good idea to head straight up to Beacon Hill before it gets too hot."

"Whatever," replied Melanee.

As they hiked uphill along the dusty, chaparral-lined trail, Dalton expounded upon some mostly forgotten local history

"It's called Beacon Hill because there used to be a beacon on the summit, which would guide planes landing at Grand Central Airport in Glendale, the main airport in L.A. during the Twenties. Howard Hughes and Charles Lindbergh used to fly out of there until they demolished it."

"Is that so?" replied Melanee.

"You can really do a lot with a little," said Dalton, changing the subject by complimenting her very casual dress. "You can get away with wearing a potato sack and make it work."

"Thanks," said Melanee, "I don't keep up with trends."

"What are we doing? What is this about?" asked Dalton, straightforwardly again changing the subject. "It's clear I like you, right? Yet, I receive mixed messages every time I see you. One moment, you let some guy at a bar drape his arm around your ass after five minutes of talking to him, the next you tell me that you want to run away with me. Where do you want to run away to? What would we be running away from?"

"Did I say that?" asked Melanee, her vision still somewhat blurred from a headache that was competing with a steadily protesting stomach. "I do want to get out of here. Did I mention that last night?"

"You told me you wanted to run away with me," replied Dalton, overcome now with an intense romantic longing for her.

"I want you to be my girlfriend for fuck sake," thought Dalton. "I don't want to horse around anymore."

"Last night, I was trashed," said Melanee befuddled. "I don't remember anything I said or did. Forgive me."

Observing the shattered look on Dalton's face, Melanee attempted to resuscitate their deeply unnatural relationship.

"I like you too, Dalton. You are a very decent guy. You haven't tried to grab my breasts and you don't get all sex crazy like some guys do. You're knowledgeable about this and that. Though, I'm not sure if I am ready to run away yet. There is a guy I like. He treats me like garbage and you've always been polite. I don't know what I want out of this life or from you. Forgive me that my heart doesn't beat loud or whatever."

"You're dating some other guy?" asked Dalton defensively.

"No, I didn't say that," replied Melanee.

She paused, not wishing to explain.

"I'm not!" she said. "I don't want to talk about it."

They hiked on, zombie-like, past an immense, somewhat industrial panorama of the city of Glendale.

"Going back to what I said before," said Dalton, catching his breath, "What are we doing then? Last night, you recited this heartfelt declaration to me that I was the sweetest, goody-good guy of all-time and you wanted to run away to a new life with me. Now, you act like you never spoke those words and there's some other dildo you're into. I'm not sure what to make of all that. Some of it has got to be phony."

"I like you, Dalton," said Melanee, exhausted and starting to become unnerved. "But I can't get beyond your tininess. I can't honestly be hot for a guy who is shorter than me. I'm like average sized. You're like Arnold. You know Arnold? The little Black kid?"

She paused trying to remember his name, as Dalton began to froth at the mouth like a rabid dog.

"Gary Coleman!" she shouted excitedly, the name of the kid actor from the Eighties TV show *Different Strokes* suddenly clicking in her brain. "You're like Gary Coleman and I'm kind of like the girl from *La Femme Nikita*, you know? We're different."

"I'm not like Gary Coleman at all! Fuck you every which way!" yelled Dalton now spitting, his temper exploding as if it were charged with dynamite.

"I didn't, I'm not ... " stammered Melanee, seeing that Dalton was red-faced and fuming. Astonished at Dalton's demoniac change of appearance and feeling like a cornered puppy, she stuck out her arm ineptly and pathetically imagining that Dalton was about to strike her. (Once, years ago, she had been decked hard when she had spoken off the cuff to René, the crook who had once employed her, and the black, swollen eye, bloody nose, and sense of humiliation had been among her shittiest life experiences.) At the same moment as she collapsed into a shielding position from Dalton, her boot hit a slippery rock propelling her farther backwards. A sheer cliff was directly behind her and she flew off it with an intensely horrific scream that seemed to last one interminable second. Then, a dull thud.

Dumbfounded, Dalton mumbled to himself, drool spilling down his chin. He peeked over the cliff. He couldn't see her.

"Where is she?" he thought, batshit crazy out of his brain. "What just happened?"

Then he spotted her. First, a red splash. Then, her body splayed gruesomely and caught in a chaparral bush, also splattered. He saw what he thought might be her brains or guts caught in the bush just below her body. He could not see her head. She was a great distance from him down a cliff that was impassable.

A deluge of sweat poured down off his head and right over the cliff in the direction of Melanee's body.

Dalton knew she was gone. His whole body was convulsing like a wet poodle. It was a jumble as to what had happened no less than a few seconds before. He felt immeasurably guilty. Then, from where he did not know, a lick of self-preservation kicked in. Any explanation he had, whatever it might be, was tenuous. Melanee was as dead as she was ever going to be and every aspect of her violent passing pointed to him perhaps killing her, not on purpose, but maybe leading her to her death somehow in some indirect manner. He'd been enraged and out of his wits. That morning, presumptuously, he had considered that by day's end Melanee might fall into his arms. But there was now no dancing around the fact that Melanee was exceedingly dead and Dalton knew he must act swiftly. He looked around him in every direction. There were distant cars on far off roads and freeways, lots of them, but he saw no one closer. Then, he noticed Melanee's black and silver bag right behind him on the trail. He yanked it up and ran.

~ 6 ~

AFTER THE FALL

Shitting ostrich-sized eggs of terror, Dalton arrived back at his car, a thermos of sweat pouring forth from his body. His very last day of freedom, he considered, could be this utterly rotten one he was now tearing through like a three-legged hyena. In his flight from the ridge from which Melanee had flown, he had passed a young couple of indiscernible foreign origins and a lone, gray-haired man with a sunburned bald spot and sunglasses. Slowing down upon passing them on the trail, he thought he might have very well looked like a crazy person, though they probably didn't notice. They might be able to identify him, but were unlikely to spy Melanee's body from the trail. Somebody below would spot it quickly, though; it may have already been discovered, he thought, panicking. He turned on the ignition and hightailed it out of Griffith Park, passing neither the police nor any emergency vehicles.

He could go home, though the idea of being trapped alone with his own conscience filled Dalton with dread. His second thought was to call Leah, but she had said she wouldn't be around. Dalton coveted friendship and companionship and at this moment, as much as ever before, he needed to share his troubles with someone. Nathan lived nearby in Los Feliz. He would know what to do next, determined Dalton. He could explain what had happened and Nathan, being one cool customer, would give him some quality advice.

Dalton pulled up in front of Nathan's duplex, hitting the curb a little hard. Pouncing from his vehicle like a possessed demon, Dalton jogged to the door praying that Nathan was in.

"Unexpected," said Nathan answering the door in an unbuttoned shirt and observing Dalton's wigged-out demeanor. "What the hell happened to you?"

"Man, some crazy stuff went down. I'm sorry just to show up here uninvited. I wasn't sure where the fuck to go."

"It's no problem really. I was just reading the paper and waiting for a phone call. Frankly, I'm not one of those people who is serene about folks dropping in, like at a barbershop, but feel free to lay whatever it is on me. Would you like something to drink?"

"Yes. Anything. And sorry again about just popping in."

"Scotch?"

"Yes, great."

"Ice?"

"Yes, please."

"Is it something with Melanee? She's unpredictable and that can be a very groovy thing a lot of the time, and then, you know, like last night she might, on occasion, do something inexplicable."

"I need to lay something on you Nathan and it's about Melanee. We're pals, right?"

"Naturally!" replied Nathan, appreciative that Dalton had called him a pal.

"Melanee is dead."

Previously buoyant upon Dalton's arrival, Nathan now registered the dull stare of someone in utter shock.

After a moment, he asked in disbelief, "Something happened last night when you left her off?"

"No," said Dalton, starting to unveil his tale trepidatiously after cooling down for a second. "Nothing much happened last night. But today I had the bright idea to go on a hike in Griffith Park, not so far from here. I wanted to catch a glimmer of reality as to where things stood. Melanee was ultimately rude, like froggy French-style, not smashed this time, so no excuse."

"I have no idea where this is going," said Nathan sternly, "but please don't tell me that you killed Melanee."

"No, no, I didn't," replied Dalton defensively. "What happened was I was worked up and suddenly she bends over like a tree in a thunderstorm at my being royally pissed. Then, I guess she slips and flies over the cliff."

"You're sure that's what occurred because it sounds fuzzy?" asked Nathan with an interrogating tone.

"It is fuzzy. Everything happened in a speck of time. I saw her body down the cliff. I meant her no harm. I never touched her."

Nathan was still visibly shaken and was struggling to process Dalton's story.

"You're sure she's dead? Did you go down the cliff or do anything to try and save her?" he asked.

"I'm not going to get into the icky details of what I saw after she fell because I can see you're wrecked about it and I feel the same way. Where her body had fallen, there was no way I could get to it and no way to save her. I was certain she was dead. The scene there, it looked like I pushed her off the cliff, but I never touched her. I booked it here. I hoped you could help me out. I promise you it was just this freak tragedy. I never meant any harm to Melanee, whatsoever. I was in love with her."

"As puzzling as that story is," replied Nathan, "I believe you. You have a stratospheric imagination, but you could not have conjured up anything so implausible to protect yourself.

You know you can rely on me. But it is a deep mire you are stuck in. You fled from the scene of a crime. Your reaction presumes guilt. Someone who witnesses a calamity like that reports it. You acted as only a murderer would."

Dalton started twitching.

"I'm going to have to ask you more questions," continued Nathan, "almost as if I were a detective because the police are probably already on this and one of the first places they are going to come is either here or your place."

"Shit, yeah, I'm sorry to get you involved," said Dalton. "I can just go to the cops."

"I don't know if I would advise that at this point. When she fell off the cliff, was there anyone around? Did anyone see you before, during, or after it happened?"

"No one saw it. We passed people on the trail."

"Did you pass any of the same people both ways?"

"I didn't notice. I don't think so."

"Did you talk to any of them?"

"No. There were a lot of people around the merry-go-round picnicking, all at a distance, though."

"Melanee was a mink of a girl. You don't think anyone noticed her?"

"Conceivably, nobody was gawking at her, like they do in bars sometimes."

"You have a couple of things in your corner, bud. It's possible nobody saw her fall. If no one can place you two together today, then it's feasible, though somewhat unlikely, that it's only me that knows you saw Melanee today. Pray that's the case."

"I swear on my Aunt Hilda's grave that no crime was committed, other than running away if that is indeed a crime."

"Was Allison there this morning?"

"No, didn't see her. She wasn't there."

"Could anyone else know that you went on a hike with Melanee today?"

"I just called her on a foolish whim and went over. I can't think of anyone."

"At Cole's last night, Melanee lit up the place like Shirley MacLaine in *Some Come Running*. It's more likely that people would have noticed me when we were leaving, rather than you because you skedaddled out of there. But people will remember her and what she looked like. Then, there's Clara, and also the bartender."

"Another thing, when Melanee went flying off that cliff, some which way or the other, she dropped her bag. It's in the car."

"Did you look through it?"

"No, I forgot about it until now."

"Go to your car, look around first, make sure no one sees you, grab the bag and bring it back here."

Dalton followed Nathan's instructions and reappeared with the bag, which Nathan unzipped.

"You've got her wallet here and her passport. That sort of changes everything," said Nathan.

"How have things changed?" asked Dalton.

"When the police find her, which they probably already have, it may not be immediate that they ID her and then come for you and me. We may have some time."

"Nathan, please help me. I'm a school teacher who gives good grades to kids when they don't deserve them. I don't want to be grilled by the police. They could probably get me to confess to assassinating John. F. Kennedy with a few pokes of a stick. Is there a way I can get out of this?"

Interrupted by a phone call, Nathan answered somewhat nervously and dismissed the person on the other line.

"Let me give you a ring later. I have someone over right now," said Nathan to the other party.

There was something unusual about the phone call, observed Dalton.

"We're both in this together," said Nathan. "We just need to be ready and calm like an ice sculpture when a squad car shows up. Melanee is alive, for all we know. Lookie here, I'm going to take care of that bag for you. Don't worry about it. You saw Melanee last night. She drank like it was some sort of contest. As for today, you have to create an alternate scenario of what you did in some other neighborhood far from Griffith Park. Don't even tell me what it is. It can't involve me. Just make it up, memorize it, and stick to it."

"That makes a lot of sense," said Dalton taking it all in. "I can't thank you enough. You're a comrade for all seasons, man. I am so sorry to drag you into this and it kills me what happened to Melanee. When it comes down to it, she was a marvel."

"She was a heartbreaker, any way you look at it," added Nathan.

"Is it wrong what we are doing?" asked Dalton. "Something seems really wicked about everything I have done since running from the scene."

"You are in a very sticky spot regardless. If you had gone to the cops just after, they would be staring you down and nobody else. I have some work I have to attend to now and some phone calls to return."

"What sort of work?" asked Dalton curiously.

"Just baloney, nothing interesting. Another thought, if they do come to you and someone has ID'd you at the scene, you might as well tell the truth. But please keep me out of it. Please don't mention me at all."

"Absolutely and thanks, I'm breathing a little bit again like a harpooned whale coming up for air."

Heretofore, Dalton's ride had been smooth, with clean contours on a steadily elevating highway. But this one spectacular accident, which he had witnessed and participated in to some degree, now derailed his every comfort. Venturing out-side of his fortress-like loft apartment building for coffee was now encumbered by the not unfounded paranoia of being hand-cuffed in front of neighbors and tossed into a hoosegow with criminals, who were sure to take issue with Dalton's disposition and height. The image of Melanee's helpless corpse could not be ripped from his conscience. His guilt was exponential, growing worse every time he had to think about it, which was every few minutes. Yet, nothing about Melanee had come up for days. It was as if she had been whitewashed from his everyday life, but continued to haunt him at all times.

In class, a student, Neil, had raised his hand and inquired inappropriately in front of the class, "Is everything okay with you, Mr. Everest? You keep blanking out in the middle of what you are saying? You have this sad look on your face."

"I have had some sleeping issues recently," replied Dal-ton. "Thank you for your concern."

A fellow teacher, Burt, his mom, and one of the baristas at the coffee shop had also queried Dalton about his sullen ex-pression, downcast eyes, and spacing out mid-sentence.

Until, finally, someone mentioned Melanee.

On the phone with Dalton, Leah asked him, "So, what ever happened with that French tart?"

"French tart?" Dalton questioned.

"Oh, I'm not referring to the pastry you picked up at La Brea Bakery. You do recall that you were obsessing about that tart and you were going to run away with her and then I never heard anything."

"That fell apart completely. Haven't seen her."

"And you're not crushed by that? You said you were in love with her. I thought you were going to turn her into your stripper wife."

"I am tore up. Melanee wasn't at all serious about me."

It was the first time he had uttered her name since the day of the accident.

"Well, if you don't want to talk about it, that's fine. It's the last thing I want to talk about. You deserve someone decent, even if you sound like a half-wit on the phone."

Upon hanging up, Dalton decided it was time to call Nathan. He was not sure why he had been putting it off. In the nastiest predicament to ever befall Dalton, Nathan had straightened him out. But he was still torn as to whether keeping his head down and pretending to himself that he was a respectable human being was the right decision. And Nathan was the only person who knew his secret, and he wasn't sure if he trusted anyone with it.

Meanwhile, Nathan had been following newspaper and TV coverage of the Griffith Park hiker Jane Doe, who had fallen from a cliff to her death. In the first couple of days, it had been among the top stories on local TV news and there had been mention of a possible homicide or suicide. The story had made the front page of the Metro section of the *L.A. Times,* though at the bottom of the page, and there had been follow up stories all centering around the unsolved identity of the girl. Police thought she might be a tourist. There were many shoe prints in the area where she had fallen. She had a tribal tattoo on her ankle and a fair amount of alcohol in her blood. Many missing person calls had come in, but none had panned out. Eventually, in the last story Nathan had read, there was no mention of a homicide or suicide. Police hoped someone would come forward with information about a missing girl.

That same day, Allison called.

"Nathan, this is Allison, Melanee's roommate. Did she go out of town? Have you seen her?"

"I haven't talked to her in days."

"I think it has been five nights since she slept here. She's never done that before. I thought maybe she was slumming it with you."

"I wonder if she just took off, went back to France," pondered Nathan. "I got the idea that she was wanting to fly the coop. She never got a job or even bothered looking for one."

"No way! She left all her crap here, just her little bag is gone."

On the evening of the day Dalton had come over, Nathan had driven out to the desert and incinerated the bag along with all of its contents.

"Maybe she just needed to leave Los Angeles, like in that X song. 'She had to get out!'" Nathan sang.

"But you were her boyfriend, correct?"

"I was not her boyfriend, incorrect."

"So, you don't care where she is?"

"I'm not going to chase after her. There are plenty of gals between here and France."

"She told me she came here with you from France."

"Yes, she did accompany me back here."

"Nathan, you handsome scoundrel," said Allison changing her tone of voice from querying to flirty. "I know there is a little goodness in that tiny iron heart of yours. Please tell me what I should do with all of her crap. She also owes me rent money."

"That's hard to say. I'm speculating that she went back to France. You could wait a little bit and see if she contacts you. If not, after a reasonable amount of time, you could take her stuff to a thrift store, and I guess, look for a new roommate."

Saying that saddened Nathan. It seemed to add even more finality to what was already very final.

"Okay," said Allison, all that Nathan had said sinking in. "I'm hurt that she would take off to France, leaving all her crap here and not even bothering to say goodbye."

"It's crummy. But that's a card Melanee might play. She doesn't strike me as the most sentimental sort. I also would have liked to say farewell."

"I could console you some time, big guy. You've got the number here. Give me a call and I promise we won't talk about Melanee at all."

"You will be hearing from me, my little blonde bad-ass."

"You don't have to give me an insipid nickname just yet."

Later that night, Dalton, unsure of where he stood with Nathan after what had happened, apprehensively gave him a call.

"Nathan, I've been meaning to ring you, but have been feeling like a heel after all that transpired."

"We should speak. Are you up to anything this evening?" asked Nathan.

"No. Do you have a place in mind?"

"How about I drop by your place, we have a talk about things, and then we'll hit up somewhere?"

"Okay," replied Dalton, his voice shrinking. "You remember where I'm at?"

"Yes, 8 pm."

This itsy-bitsy making of plans made Dalton shiver because of its irregularity. Nearly every time they had hung out, Nathan wanted to meet late at a bar. Why, he fretted, would Nathan, who had only been to his loft once before when he had insisted he come over while half smashed, want to show up at his pad and discuss "things"? This ominous change in routine caused Dalton's intestines to twist about like the animal balloons of a demented clown. Something was amiss and Dalton did not know then, since it was frequent that he would freak out about this or that, that on this occasion he had good reason to be terrified.

Buzzing Nathan into the entry gate on the first floor, Dalton hid an embarrassing book he was reading, *Memoirs of a Geisha*, which his mom had lent him. Mechanically, he checked his fly, which was closed. Then he decided to dim the lights for no particular reason. He was fond of playing with the dimmer.

A knock at the door and Dalton gulped. Some indeterminate bad news could be waiting on the other side. Nathan entered, all smiles, glad to see him.

"Things look to have blown over," said Nathan.

"What do you mean?" asked Dalton, not containing his fear.

"The fuzz haven't figured out the first thing. They have no idea who Melanee is. You've read the papers, right?"

"No, I've been avoiding all media. Didn't look at anything."

"Really?"

Nathan paused a little stunned by the inanity of Dalton blocking out all information, but then conceded to himself that perhaps that was sensible.

"The course I had suggested," continued Nathan, "to lay low, not talk to anyone, go about your usual routines, was the correct one. Had you headed to the cops with that wishy-washy story after skipping the crime scene, as you said you might, you would likely be eating stale biscuits with a guy named Luther right now."

Exhaling, Dalton began to loosen up, realizing that Nathan was the bearer of heartening news.

"Man, I owe you a thousand times over. I was feeling like I was already dead and buried. I'm buying tonight, multiple rounds."

"Thanks, no need. I have a little enterprise in mind and I think you're perfect for it, chief."

"Don't tell me you're a Scientologist?"

"God no," said Nathan.

"It's not a pyramid scheme. You don't want me to sell Herbalife, do you?" joked Dalton.

"Nope. I rob houses, rich people. It's amazing the amount of junk that some of them have that they don't necessarily need. I sell their stuff to clients of mine, some of whom I've been working with for years. It's mostly late night, a few hours here and there, easy doings. For now, I need you to help with the driving and such, nothing too stressful. I can train you on the job. Eventually, though, I want you to be a sort of partner. You will never want for anything again. You could even wave goodbye to the teaching. I may not present myself as someone who is in the chips, but I live very comfortably."

Dumbstruck at this proposal, Dalton eased into an answer.

"I don't know that I'm the ideal thief. I've never shoplifted anything in my life. Robbing people, it's just not something I would do. I don't have a problem ... if that's what you do. But I'm not going to be party to breaking into anyone's home, whether they're filthy, moneyed scumbags or not. I thank you for thinking of me. We're great drinking buddies."

"I have not come to the decision to let you in on this lightly," continued Nathan. "You are suited for this work. There aren't a whole lot of people you can trust in this world. I was there to handle the situation when you were wedged in a really bad spot. I need you to spend a few late evening hours with me not drinking, but driving around some fancy Westside neighborhoods. The car we're driving in, it won't always be my car. You'll get the hang of the whole thing quick as a cricket."

Nathan pulled out his wallet, gave Dalton a smile, which Dalton thought was a wee bit creepy, and started piling up crisp hundred dollar bills on a table next to the sofa.

"There's three grand. I just need you to meet up with me at 2 am tomorrow night for a couple hours. I'll explain everything then."

"Crime, it's not for me," mumbled Dalton staring at the money. "I think you've got the wrong person."

"Rather than going out, why don't we have a drink here?" asked Nathan. "Have you got anything?"

"Sure, sure," said Dalton, all nerves. "I've got vodka, Bacardi."

"Vodka with ice, water or soda is fine. Whatever you've got."

Dalton had some ornate glasses he had inherited from a great aunt. He added ice to the vodka.

"Orange soda?" asked Dalton.

"No thanks," replied Nathan.

Dalton added some Sunkist orange soda to his drink.

They sat down on a white Ikea couch.

The plan had always been a bit screwy, Nathan pondered to himself. He had figured if Melanee could win Dalton's heart and she was working for him, he could get Dalton, who he considered a major pushover, to be the ideal hyper-intelligent cohort. Nathan had never had a partner before who wasn't already enmeshed in some way in the world of criminality and every one of them had turned out a screw up. Javier had been a cruel, unreliable asshole with a long rap sheet whose internal compass would always point him toward prison. He had almost thought he would have to kill Javier to be rid of him, but then he had gotten picked up on something unrelated to any of their jobs. Zeke was a Hollywood druggie whose only positive traits were his quickness at running away with other people's property and his absolutely not giving a shit about any consequences. He might have guessed that Zeke would try to sell their winnings for his own profit. And from the very start, he realized Melanee wasn't cut out for high-end thievery. He had just gotten to like her so much. When they worked together, he imagined her to be by his side in a Jean-Pierre Melville film. But she had never driven a car in her life and the single time she had broken into a house, she had left her bag there, that same bag that he had burned. He had to sneak into the house again in broad daylight to retrieve it.

Aside from the fact that he really enjoyed Dalton's company and needed someone bright and less crooked, he was unerring that his offer would turn Dalton's life around. He just had to make Dalton see the whole canvas for what it was, or the more attractive parts of it, which was essentially the wads of dough and the thrill of making it in that fashion. He couldn't get into the details just yet, as some of them were sure to turn off the uninitiated. No matter what though, he wasn't leaving without Dalton's submission to his plan.

"This offer is exclusive to you, brother, a ticket to sitting pretty," said Nathan.

Reverting quickly to being a wreck, Dalton downed the Vodka and Sunkist with voracious thirst. This sharp unexpected turn had him pinned on the floor. Dalton had no desire to steal. There had never been a thought in his head on the subject. But he found himself mulling it over, contemplating how to say no like he meant it, but at the same time was unable to remove the stack of bills sitting on the table out of his deliberations.

Silently, he drank and then poured himself another one, while Nathan, who had barely touched his drink, remained his usual calm self.

"I'm all for living high off the hog," said Dalton shakily. "I understand the appeal of making a lot of fast money. But you know I'm into teaching, for the most part. The money isn't terrible. It could be better. I have some job security. I'm not the sort of risk taker that you are."

"Keep teaching," replied Nathan. "But what I am talking about, it's like going on a rollercoaster or eating ice cream for the first time or when a girl finally agrees to have sex with you. You get all tingly, but in this case, you stay that way."

Nathan could tell by Dalton's minutely intrigued expression that he had turned a corner. He wasn't even sure how he had done it. At any rate, Dalton couldn't pass up all the money he had laid out. He had made robbing houses sound like going to the circus. It was a stretch, but there was that aspect of gleeful pillaging, which was not dissimilar from being an adolescent rascal.

"Fine," Dalton yielded, not even sure how it happened. "I agree to meet up with you tomorrow night. But I won't steal anything and I won't commit any crime that would get me fired from my job. I just want a look-see."

"Meet me at my place at 2."

~ 7 ~

A FEW MISGIVINGS

An intimidating voice, clearly suspicious and inches away from Dalton said, "I need to know what you guys are doing here."

Casing a house, though it was unseen behind a stone wall, a couple of trees and massive hedges, Nathan and Dalton had been sitting in Dalton's Honda on Lloydcrest Drive off Coldwater Canyon discussing the fundamentals of larceny in the dead of night. Nathan had been describing Dalton's role as the driver as "doing almost nothing" and "painless." But as Dalton voiced objections and simultaneously showed interest by inquiring further about Nathan's plans, a man inaudibly snuck up from behind them in the pitch dark and appeared at Dalton's window.

"Sorry to bother you sir," replied Nathan in a reassuring voice, which sounded not much like how he usually spoke. "We were just talking, having a little argument. Were we being noisy?"

Nathan was sure they had been whispering. The man, not police or security, because he was not wearing a uniform, must have heard them pull up.

"You don't live around here, do you? Are you staying around here?" demanded the man.

"No sir," replied Nathan. "We were just cruising around in the hills and stopped here to have a conversation."

In the darkness, both Dalton and Nathan now caught a glimpse of the man. He was a big fellow, hair mostly gray, resembling George Lucas, though scruffier.

"Look, I'm aware the Rodriguezes are out of town. I've been taking care of their cat and looking after their house. I'm going to memorize your license plate number and then write it down when I'm inside. Then, I am going to call the police. While I do that, I suggest you get out of this neighborhood and don't come back if you know what's good for you."

"Hey big shot," said Dalton, shifting from fright to insolence, speedily. "You're not the mayor of this street just because you are feeding someone's cat. We have every right to sit here peacefully and have a private conversation. We don't give a whiff about the Rodriguezes."

"I saw you trying to peer over that wall. If you're thinking of going in there, I'll have the police here before you step out of the car."

"Sir," said Nathan trying to keep the situation from unraveling by repeatedly calling the man sir. "We have no interest in that house. I apologize for waking you at this hour. " Looking at Dalton, "Okay, let's leave."

Dalton turned on the ignition and lights and they could finally see the full figure of the man in pink shorts with big hairy legs and an extra-large black T-shirt staring at Dalton's license plate. The man got out of their way and they headed downhill toward Sunset Boulevard.

"That scheme is cooked," commented Nathan.

"I'd say," replied Dalton. "Am I in the shitter now? Are the police going to come after me, after this doofus gives them my license plate number?"

"No chance of that. Our neighborly chum is unlikely to call the police because he's got nothing on us and if he does call them, what would they do with your license plate number? Were we committing a crime? No."

"You're sure of that?"

"He's got zilch. He was just trying to scare us away and he attained that goal."

"What was with the polite routine if this jerkamabob can do nothing to us?"

"Did we have any reason to get into it with this guy?" asked Nathan. "I mean I know you are a bad-ass. If you recall, there was that one time, maybe a couple of months ago, when we were at The Ski Room and there was this middle-aged ex-punk guy that we got into a rambling conversation with. All of us were shellacked and you came up with this whole racket where you claimed you were the rapper, Kid Frost, which was very funny, since he's Latino."

Dalton chuckled at the memory.

"He didn't think it was that funny because he was a dope and he thought you were lying to him or something. You said 'no 8X10 headshot for you.' Then the guy started to pour a beer on your head and you gave him a shove that knocked him on his rear. He was still blathering. But you held your ground and didn't let it turn into anything, which I admired because there was no rationale to beat the stuffing out of that moron, though had you wanted to, you could have. I could tell as much."

"Thanks Nathan, really. It's true. I have been in some scraps over the years and the other guy ended up lying flat. I have some boxing and martial arts experience."

"It's a roundabout way of saying that in this line of work being secure that you can thrash someone if need be is an asset, but in just about any given situation, the best course is to lay off or get out. This oaf ruined the score, but to get into it with him served no purpose except to attract the police."

"Sure. I see that. Makes sense. But to be as candid as Oprah with you, breaking into houses seems like a massive ass-load of risk to me and I'm risk averse, I swear."

"I can't remember the last time I had any dealings with a hostile neighbor," reckoned Nathan as they drove down the Sunset Strip, which was bright lights, but entirely dead at this hour. "I never bump into cops or security patrols. I have a couple of guys I pay off at Bel Air Patrol and Westec. It makes the goings easy."

"So, you've never done any time?"

"No, no real time. Juvie, a few months of juvie. Only one arrest when I was an adult and they couldn't make it stick."

"And you're not afraid of jail?"

"I'm good at what I do, and I'm not planning on being sent up anytime soon."

"Still, I don't know. Not sure why you think I would be any good at this."

"Want to see something that will knock your socks off?"

"Sure."

"Okay, when we hit the 101, take it north. I've got something to show you. It's in Sun Valley."

"I have to get up for school tomorrow."

"School can wait. This cannot."

In a distant, industrial corner of the San Fernando Valley, they turned into a darkened storage unit building, parked and then walked upstairs into a dank, unlighted corridor. Nathan switched on a tiny flashlight and pulled out a set of keys, opening a very small unit.

"Open sesame!" said Nathan shining his flashlight into the unit.

Nathan began opening jewelry boxes which contained diamonds and exquisite designer jewelry. There were also Rolex watches, a gorgeous art deco vase wrapped in some paper and several paintings.

"By the beard of Zeus!" exclaimed Dalton with his mouth agape. "Are those real diamonds?"

"They are. All of it is hot property, stuff that sits here and collects dust. I'm not sure what to do with all of it. It's too risky to sell."

"Man, the paintings?"

"This is a Llyn Foulkes. It's worth a hell of a lot. But I should have left it on the wall. It's not worth anything to me. And the other one is a hotshot painter, don't remember the name. I can't sell either of them. The artist is a little too well known."

"I mean, you could return the stuff to the owners, couldn't you? You could mail the jewelry back. That seems safe. I don't imagine they could trace it."

"There is some sense to that, but if I may be frank, I don't remember where most of it came from. That huge diamond ring, I stole that four or five years ago, somewhere in Bel Air. I don't remember which house, no clue. Tell you what, if anything catches your eye, take anything you want, just don't ever try and sell it."

Dalton was astonished at this offer. He considered that the paintings would look swell on his wall, but maybe displaying stolen art at his pad was a numbskull idea. He didn't care for Rolex watches. But owning a diamond was unexpectedly appealing. Should he own a stolen diamond, he wondered, was that a bright idea? Wasn't he finding himself more and more enmeshed in this odd new career Nathan had chosen for him?

"Don't be shy," encouraged Nathan. "I really don't know what to do with any of it."

"This stash has to be worth millions."

"Something like that," said Nathan showing off.

"I can't really think of an argument against a free diamond, stolen from some Beverly Hills housewife, I imagine. Would it be kosher if I took this ring?"

The engagement ring, a medium-sized diamond set amongst smaller diamonds in a petal setting on a gold band, was more tasteful than some of the other jewelry.

"It's yours. Good choice," said Nathan, closing the unit, Dalton placing the five-thousand-dollar ring into his Levi's pocket.

It was 4 am as they drove back to Los Feliz, passing a few cars on the freeway.

"I know you're from L.A., but where exactly did you grow up?" asked Dalton, who in the past had given up on asking Nathan much of anything about his life, but was as curious as ever and had discerned Nathan was now more forthcoming.

"I was born in Fontana."

"Fontana?" exclaimed Dalton. "Is that in L.A. County? I don't even know where Fontana is."

"It's between San Bernardino and Rancho Cucamonga and there isn't much there, no reason to go there ever, but that's where I grew up. When I was in junior high, my dad got to moving around. I lived out in El Monte, Whittier, and one year in Echo Park, dropped out of school that year. The gangs in the neighborhood were more stimulating. I had been barely attending school anyways."

"But you're one well-educated dropout."

"Didn't have anything to do with my dad or school. In my early twenties, I took it upon myself to become well read."

"I noticed the bookshelf at your pad."

"Because of my line of work, I've had no shortage of reading time. I wouldn't pretend it's the sort of learning that you've had, going to a prestigious university and obtaining a degree, but I figure I also have a lot I can teach, in the school of hard knocks or whatever."

They both laughed.

Really though, Nathan's story was much grimmer than he would ever let on to anyone. It was a narrative that he guarded because it possessed no silver lining. On only two occasions in his life had he revealed his childhood story, once to his seventh grade English teacher, and another time to a girl named Lopita; both had been shocked and nearly speechless.

Nathan had no memory of his mom, Mona. He had first visited her grave in San Bernardino when he was 16. He knew that she had been a druggie and he had heard that she had sold drugs. His dad, Garrett, would never say a kind word about her.

"You're lucky you never knew her," his dad had said more than once.

He had been raised from as early as he could remember by his paternal grandmother, Gael, a cold, dispassionate woman who seemed to resent the job. They lived in a tiny studio apartment in Fontana and were dirt poor, the little money they had coming from a mysterious source.

When Nathan was perhaps eleven or so, his father appeared for the first time, ostensibly let out of prison after a long stretch. Nathan remembered the first time they met. He was in awe of this man he had not always believed to be a real person. Nathan went unacknowledged for a couple of days, until his father wanted to crash on the sofa while Nathan was watching cartoons. His memories of the next period of his life were murky. His father and grandmother argued violently. He was taken away, never to see his grandmother again. There was a long period where he didn't go to school and moved around, he and his dad crashing at the apartments of various lowlifes, some bad, some memorably awful.

After being left to his own devices and having next to no social contact for most of his childhood, Nathan was at one point suddenly recognized as verifiable offspring by his father and so began his curious education. This change came about when his father had hauled in a big score and they had moved to an apartment of their own in El Monte.

His dad, who up to that point had spoken to him as little as possible, had given him a sort of speech about how things were going to be.

"Listen kid," his father had said, never calling him by his name. "You're not going to make it in this world. There's no woman around to care for you. Your grandma's dead."

Nathan was old enough to assume that was a lie. His grandmother had not been sick or elderly. She just didn't want him around anymore.

"I don't want you to end up as a piece of trash or a nimrod and it looks like you're headed in that direction," his father continued in his customary insulting manner. "I may not always be around, so I'm going to teach you how to survive. I'm going to start sending you to school, but I don't know what they'll teach you there. I never learned much at school, but maybe you will, or maybe you won't learn anything. Anyways, the neighbors will call the authorities if they don't see you going to school, and I don't need the attention. How to make a dime, though, without any bosses ordering you around, that schooling is going to be my little favor to you."

His father became the captivating focal point of Nathan's existence. He was a mean son of a bitch, unremittingly cynical, and cruelly honest. But his lessons stuck. Nathan learned how to shoplift everything. He was a natural. He watched his father, from the door of the pool room, hustle dough.

In the back room of a pizza place in West Covina, his father instructed him in the game, and Nathan obsessed over it, taking his first dollar from a kid on a pool bet at the age of thirteen. When his father began to notice that Nathan had a knack for it, they started breaking into houses together. Nathan was nimble, meticulous, and fearless. His father showed him how to climb walls, pick locks, disable alarms, pacify dogs, rob places blind and sell the merchandise to fences. Nathan drank it all up like a Slurpee. He had finally found his calling as a human being.

Living in Echo Park, aged fourteen, and for the most part independent, Nathan, caught up in his delinquent lifestyle of smoking weed, trying to make it with cholitas and petty thievery, lost track of his dad, who often disappeared for weeks. One day, hung over and sound asleep, Nathan heard a loud banging at the door. An older woman, Lois, claiming to be a cousin insisted on being let in, and her hard-as-nails exterior was certainly that of the Lyme clan. She told Nathan that his father had been killed, providing no details. A family member, an aunt or something, whom Nathan had never met had recruited Lois to be his guardian. Lois' son was grown up and out of the house. Nathan would have to come live with her and her husband, Roy, in Ontario, a town that was quite a ways east of L.A. He protested, but she insisted he would be kicked out of the apartment by the landlord and put in a foster home. She turned out to be a horrendous cook and a lackadaisical guardian, which suited Nathan, while her husband, Roy, was an outright nincompoop. However, Nathan had had enough of living in the boondocks. It took him a full year to get enough cash together robbing the neighbors so that he could finally head out on his own.

Struggling at first, Nathan lived at a gang hangout in the Rampart District of L.A., not far from Downtown. It was a flop house for members who were in and out of jail. But the gang, known as Barrio 18, didn't have much use for Nathan, whose presence was only tolerated because he was so adept at thievery and because the others thought it was amusing to have a white dude around who they nicknamed Iceman, after the *Top Gun* character. After a few weeks, he'd been arrested in a gang sweep and knew he had to set up shop on his own. Managing to rent an apartment nearby, Nathan's career trajectory was mostly straight up from there.

Over the years, Nathan had become more confident and educated, better dressed and well spoken. But the inheritance of his lack of upbringing left him with certain social limitations that he had a hell of a time overcoming. One piece of questionable advice that his dad had offered him went something like, "Don't get too close to people. Bob and Tina, or whoever, will not approve of what it is we do. You will always need a cover. No one ever needs to know what you're about, what you do."

Nathan often sang to himself the Germs song, "What We Do is Secret."

But even for a crook, Nathan's was a lonely soul. He had never managed to have a normal relationship with a girl and was not at all keen on any form of romance. If a girl were to try to hold his hand, Nathan would write her off entirely.

Recently, it had been a revelation to Nathan that friendship was also something he had generally lacked and avoided for a lifetime. Almost every pseudo friendship he had managed was tied inexorably to crime. He had decided that the only way he could become true pals with Dalton was to haul him wholesale into his world. He could turn Dalton into a thief like himself and once a thief, Nathan could share anything on his mind with Dalton. It was what he imagined real friends did. And to be pals like that, Nathan believed he had to make Dalton more like himself. Anybody might have told him that that was a shit-for-brains idea, but no one told him that because Nathan had no other friends to speak of.

Back at Nathan's place, they parted ways.

"I don't have anything coming up, no current plans for jobs right now," said Nathan stepping out of Dalton's car and speaking through the window. "But opportunities arrive unexpectedly and often, so you will hear from me."

"I'm still on the fence about the whole thing," replied Dalton. "I don't know if I want to spice my life up like it's Korean barbecue."

"I'm not sure if you should compare your life to spicy beef or if one should speak of adding spice to their life as a metaphor, ever," said Nathan, straight-faced.

Though Dalton had repeated his circumspection about pursuing a life of crime, the realization was starting to smack him in the face that he was fully drawn in and fascinated with everything that had happened that evening. When Nathan had first mentioned that he robbed houses, Dalton had believed him, but had had a very difficult time visualizing the whole scenario. After seeing Nathan's stash of riches that were too hot to sell, it was obvious that his friend was a legitimate and wildly successful crook. It was all a little unbelievable, but very real now. That tingly feeling that Nathan had mentioned already seemed to be having its way with Dalton. He may have never dreamt of a life that was in any way daring or on the edge, but there was now one readily available, and, in fact, beckoning him and offering him infinite sweets.

Four days later, Dalton received a semi-urgent message on his answering machine. Come over right away, Nathan insisted. Jumping on the 101 freeway, Dalton hit awful, late rush hour traffic. He got off at Glendale Boulevard, but again found himself proceeding at an old man with a walker's pace past the Echo Park Lake and then again when he made a left onto Sunset.

"You can't leave your truck sticking out of a driveway in the middle of Sunset Boulevard just because you are the proud owner of an orange cone," Dalton railed to himself as his car inched around the truck.

Nathan had said he'd be there at 8:30 and it was 8:25. In a desperate attempt at a shortcut he had not previously tried, he cut down to Silver Lake Boulevard and made a left on Effie Street, driving up and down the Silver Lake hills in order to save a few minutes driving time.

Ultimately, he arrived 20 minutes late.

"Sorry, I hit some unforgiving traffic on the way," apologized Dalton, sweating and manic.

"No matter," replied Nathan. "We're not in a hurry."

Dalton sighed. His tremendous effort navigating savage traffic had been for little glory, as had been the case so often before.

"I don't want to take my car after that dildo mentioned writing down my license plate."

"No problem, panty-waist. We can grab mine. In just a little bit, though, you're going to be driving my car and I'm going to be driving someone else's car."

Nathan drove west on Franklin Avenue into East Hollywood. Close to Normandie, he slowed down and began peering at parked cars on the side of the road. He then pulled into a spot and parked.

"I'm going to grab that Nissan Sentra back there. It will probably take me a minute or two. Once you see me pull out, meet me in the Rite Aid parking lot, just a block south of Franklin on Western. You can follow me."

"Whoa! You're stealing that car?"

"No, it's my cousin Harry's car," replied Nathan sarcastically. "He said I could borrow it any time. Yes, I am going to steal it."

Nathan leapt out of the car.

"Get in the driver's seat!" he instructed Dalton.

In Nathan's rearview mirror, he saw Nathan slim jimmying his way into the car. Then he was inside. 20 seconds later, Nathan pulled out and Dalton followed him to the Rite Aid.

Nathan parked the car next to him, jumped into the passenger's seat of his own car and said, "Let's scram!"

"What was that about?" asked Dalton.

"We are going to use that Nissan later tonight. I just wanted to make sure we had a car ready to go and parked nearby. We've got many hours to kill now, so what say we head downtown to Hank's and have a drink, just one or two. We want to be completely sober tonight for this job. On the way, I will give you the scoop. Of course, we won't talk about it when we get there, only in the car."

"Man, I've got a stack of homework to grade tonight."

"Couldn't you tell your students that your dog ate their homework?"

"Okay, Mr. Cool Guy Thief. Fuck the kids! Crime before children. Tell me about this job," replied Dalton.

"It's a house way up on a mountain in Pasadena on Glen Oaks Boulevard. It's not that easy to find and very quiet there. I dropped by last night to scope it out. It looks like one guy lives there. He's an Art Center professor who is out of town just 'till tomorrow. He's in Zurich."

"How did you figure all that?"

"I have a travel agent who gives me tips. I pay him probably ten times what the travel agency pays him, so he's been very loyal, a real peach. He gives me the return flight times and the address. I got the other info about this guy by flipping through his mail. There's always a chance that there's a girlfriend or someone else who lives there. It's unlikely, no other names on the mail. Nobody was there last night, one car."

"So, I am driving the stolen car?"

"Yes, tonight, your job is to drive the car we stole to Pasadena. If nobody finds it in the Rite Aid parking lot, and it's likely no one will because who is going to be looking for it there, and so then it stands to reason that absolutely no one will be looking for it on some isolated street on the edge of Pasadena. So, no worries. This one's a cinch. You'll park in the driveway of the house."

"Because this is your first caper," Nathan continued, "I have to warn you about the variable possibilities of things that may never occur, like preparing an airplane pilot for improbable disasters."

"Okay. Go ahead, shoot," said Dalton, knowing he was all the way in now or far enough that he would have to grin and bear it.

"If someone were to drive up and try to get into the driveway while you were parked there and I'm in the house, book it immediately, leave the car three or four blocks from my house, don't let anyone see you getting out of the car and meet me at my place, and I'll be there when I get there. I will give you a key tonight and I have a couple of cell phones that we'll only use while on a job. So, if this were to happen, this car coming up, you'd have to beat it out of there quickly, and the very second you're free of them, you need to call me on your cell phone and tell me to get out of there. If all this were to go down, which it won't, I'm on my own. I will have to hide my tools somewhere and find my way back to my house by taxi or whatever. I may call you and come up with a rendezvous spot. Got it?"

"I guess. I've never used a cell phone before. My friend Audrey has one."

"OK, well, we will only talk to each other with them and only while on a job. If we are going to use them for this, we can't use them otherwise."

"Makes sense."

"If a private security car comes by, same thing, except keep an eye on whether he follows you or stays at the house. If he's following you, go slow at first, just drive normal. He's not a cop. If he continues behind you or he calls the cops and you hear sirens, you will have to lose him. He's not going to chase you all over town. Once you're sure he is gone, you might consider ditching the car. I'm not going to pretend that I haven't been spotted by private security before. It's not a big deal. You just get out of there quickly. They don't want to follow you as much as you want to get away. In this part of Pasadena that doesn't have many houses, probably there is no private security, but I can't be sure. This guy doesn't have an alarm and that's usually a sign that he hasn't thought much about protecting his house. A worst case scenario is that the police could show up while you are on a job."

"Has that happened to you?" asked Dalton.

"Once or twice."

"Once or twice?" asked Dalton, confounded.

View-Master-like images of the six occasions when the police had arrived during a job popped up in Nathan's brain.

"Twice," Nathan stated emphatically. "The one time they didn't see me at all. This other time, there was a short chase and I ran away, leaving the car there. It was scary, but once I was clear of the coppers, I felt like James Cagney."

"Doesn't James Cagney climb up a tower until they shoot him and then he falls off and yells something to his mom?"

"They had the Hays Code in Hollywood back then. Gangsters always bit the dust."

"So, if you're in a residential area in the middle of the night," Nathan continued, "the police are not going to casually drive by. If you spot them, somebody called them or an alarm was tripped. You need to floor it and then ditch the car and travel on foot as soon as you possibly can. Really, it's not going to happen, but I have to prepare you for any scenario. You would want to ditch the car before they summon a helicopter. Finding a good hiding place for yourself distant from the ditched car is the best way to go. When the sun comes up, they will not be looking for a car thief or even a house thief. Cops have better things to do. But you don't want to get into a car chase with the cops. If you do, you're chopped liver."

"So you don't carry a weapon?"

"I don't carry a gun on jobs. That adds a whole other element that makes it all the more grave if you walk into something unexpected. I don't need that option. I'm not going to point a gun at someone and rob them or point a gun at a security patrol guy. That's only going to turn out badly. Frankly, I hate everything about guns and America's obsession with them. However, once in a blue moon, when you are selling stolen goods, you do need to be armed. With a familiar client, there is no need for a weapon. But once in a while, you can make a lot more money by dealing with someone that you know much less about. And sometimes, in those cases, it is a good idea to carry a piece. You, my friend, will not be carrying one, unless you want to of course."

"Oh no. I don't know the first thing about guns. I am a school teacher first and foremost."

They both enjoyed some hearty laughter as they parked on Grand Avenue down the street from Hank's Bar, a dive that attracted a mostly older crowd of folks who came after work to socialize and get blitzed. Nathan and Dalton entered the darkness of the bar area, grabbing a couple of stools. The lady bartender smelled strongly of alcohol, while a noisily festive group of boozed-up regulars was sprawled about the tiny, unadorned barroom bragging and blabbing.

Without trying, Nathan and Dalton found themselves drawn into a conversation about L.A. led by a New Yorker, who was in L.A. on business and complaining about the city to the bar's mixed bag of drunkards.

"This city is great if you are into rollerblading in purple short shorts with your headphones on," said the well-dressed man slurring the occasional word, "not as good if you value real conversation with down-to-Earth people who don't have alfalfa sprouts for brains."

"But sir," said a young Black man seated between the New Yorker and Nathan, "look who you are talking to. I was born and raised here and I don't ride around on no rollerblades. I'm just a regular person like you."

"Of course, you are," said the New Yorker. "But I'm not talking about you per se. I'm speaking of the guy in a red German sports car zipping around with his hair all windblown. This jackass thinks he's giving back to the community by tossing money at this cause or the other. He loves Bill Clinton and shitty classic rock and he's a superficial dickhead."

"I don't see that guy as the ambassador of Los Angeles," said Nathan jumping into the conversation. "He exists, but it's more of a belabored stereotype than someone you are going to run into."

"A Latino, some African-Americans, this Asian fellow," said Nathan gesturing to each person seated at the bar, "my friend Dalton here and I are a more accurate reflection of the city. You could probably find a similar group of miscellany in a bar in New York, except the accents might be a tad stronger and there could be the odd Puerto Rican."

"But there's so much not to like about Los Angeles," the New Yorker went on. "You can't get anywhere without a car, and taxis are an out of this world rip-off. If you want to get to Santa Monica, it's an hour and a half away in bumper to bumper traffic. It's not even worth it. And then when you get there, you've arrived in this sort of ugly place where fake new age mysticism reigns. It's like a shopping mall full of Zen rubbish. There's the ocean, okay, I give you that. But the people are like lettuce-munching health zombies."

The cheery, handsome Latino at the far end of the bar burst into horse laughter at this assertion.

"What are you talkin' about?" he managed to say through furious gusts of chortling.

"I like the Zen rubbish," said a Black man wearing a bright lobster colored suit and with white headphone cords coming out of his ears, sitting on the other side of the New Yorker. "I don't know what it means, but I like the sound of it."

"I'm not going to defend Santa Monica," argued Nathan, "but driving in L.A. is one of the recurring pleasures of living here, which no amount of dreary subway riding could ever surpass."

"Nonsense!" spouted the New Yorker. "It's purgatory on Earth trying to get anywhere. I wouldn't call it driving. You're basically parked in the middle of the street surrounded by other cars moving an inch at a time."

"I doubt you've ever driven the freeways at night here when they are deserted," countered Nathan, feathers ruffled, "or leisurely taken the curves of Sunset Boulevard, or rode the PCH beyond Malibu, or cruised down the 110 along the Arroyo Seco to Pasadena. Any of those experiences beats a piss-smelling subway or a cigarette-scented taxi."

"Damn straight!" added the young Black man, seated between the New Yorker and Nathan.

"The subway can get you from Uptown to Brooklyn in twenty minutes," said the New Yorker refusing to back down despite the room beginning to turn on him. "It's an efficient system, not a soul killer like L.A. traffic."

A second glass of Scotch with ice was starting to hit Nathan straight in the gourd as he fantasized about snuffing the life out of his relentlessly insufferable adversary from New York, who would never give an inch.

Nathan and Dalton departed from Hank's with the man still hitting the same notes. They took the 101 back to Nathan's pad, where Nathan gave Dalton a cell phone, which he asked him to return at the end of the night.

At around 1:30 am, they drove back to the Rite-Aid parking lot, which was deserted, the stolen car sitting by itself. They parked Nathan's car on Franklin and jumped into the stolen Nissan, Nathan instructing Dalton on how to easily restart it with a screwdriver, as he placed some boxes and garbage bags on the back seat. Once the car was started, Nathan got out again to check that all the lights were functioning.

"You don't need to be hyper-alert while driving a stolen car," explained Nathan as they drove down Los Feliz Boulevard hitting green lights. "Cops spend a minimum amount of time looking for stolen cars. I know you're a good driver who probably never gets pulled over. You just have to drive in that same relaxed fashion. If a cop pulls up next to us at a stop light, act normal."

"I got a ticket once for driving with my lights off," said Dalton, "and a speeding ticket in my first months of driving. I got a parking ticket in Glendale a couple of weeks ago for parking my car in the opposite direction of the other parked cars. But thank you for suggesting that I am better than that. I think so."

"Make sure you pay that ticket," said Nathan. "It's that sort of detail that has tripped up your Al Capones and such."

Getting off at the Colorado Boulevard exit in Pasadena, rather than earlier as they had meant to, Nathan and Dalton had to backtrack their way to Glen Oaks Boulevard using a map that Nathan had in his tool box and then follow the curvy road past a splendid mountaintop panorama of Los Angeles.

"Check out this sci-fi looking house on the right," pointed out Nathan, as if he was giving a guided tour. "This street is a mecca of supercool modernism, as opposed to the rest of Pasadena, which is famous for Craftsman houses."

They arrived at the two-story Spanish bungalow and pulled as far into the driveway as they could, backing up right next to the house.

"I really can't tell you how long this is going to take," said Nathan, adrenalin kicking in. "Just sit tight."

Time moving at the speed of the second hand on Dalton's watch, he sat fitfully in the stolen car ruminating on his current circumstances. He had expected to be jumpier. Rationally, it was improbable that the cops would appear. Nathan seemed more with it and wary of consequences than he could have ever imagined. After all, it was conceivable that Nathan was someone Dalton could count on, despite being a criminal. With this newfound optimism, he became reasonably calm. He began considering what he might have for lunch the next day. He was awfully fond of a burrito stand near his school, which was patronized by both teachers and students. But perhaps he might go to the new-ish coffeehouse, which also made froufrou sandwiches. He had been there only once and thought the BLT with caramelized onions was out of this world.

Suddenly, Nathan opened the passenger door arousing Dalton from his humdrum thoughts.

"Pop the trunk," he ordered.

Nathan was carrying two huge garbage bags filled with loot.

"Let's peel out of here," he said entering the car out of breath. "All went smooth as silk."

While heading back to Los Feliz, Nathan gleefully explained how it had gone.

"Naturally, this art professor had a lot of contemporary art around his place, but I haven't had much luck unloading that sort of stuff, so I ignored it. But our pal was also into all the latest technology and I found what I think is a serious comic book collection. There was no way I could grab all of it, but what I grabbed I could tell was collectible stuff by some of the price tags on the plastic. Since I felt we had all the time in the world, I went through every drawer in the house. I don't remember what I took, but there was plenty."

They arrived back on Franklin leaving the stolen car a few cars down from where Nathan's Audi was parked. Nathan then heaved the two tremendous double bags and several boxes of stolen loot and dumped them in his trunk.

"The last piece of business is to leave our treasure at my storage unit in Vernon."

"Vernon?" exclaimed Dalton. "Why not Fontana?"

"I have a unit in Fontana. The Vernon one is more convenient."

"There is something about you that is very Fontana, you must admit, Nathan?"

"You can make fun of Fontana all you like. Until you've lived there, you don't know the half. It's easiest then to drop by my place and have you pick up your car. Then, we'll drop your car at your place and proceed to Vernon, which is ten minutes or so from your loft."

"Vernon is only ten minutes or so from my loft? No way."

"Yes, it is, and that is the kind of useless factoid that all true Angelenos should carry around in their back pocket."

Driving through the cement and steel industrial nowheresville of Vernon in the early am, Nathan and Dalton passed a Latina lady on the sidewalk with four unleashed Chihuahuas twirling around her legs.

"I guess they needed to get out," commented Nathan.

They stopped at Pacific Storage, the sun commencing to peek out from the horizon. Dalton could not handle either of the bags on his own, so the two of them struggled with each bag balancing them up a narrow flight of cement stairs. Nathan mentioned that there was a camera in the elevator, so the stairs were the only safe option. The storage unit was large and mostly empty, except for a curious collection of matching all wooden German antiques, a clock, a chest, a mirror, and a small cabinet.

"I don't know what to do with those," said Nathan. "If someone would give me $200 for the lot, I would take it."

"That's good looking polished wood."

"I would offer it to you, but I don't think it would work in your place."

"No, but it would look great at my grandma's house."

"One thing about house robbery," said Nathan, "is that it is really not on the radar of news organizations or the cops. Your local TV news covers crime like it's the only thing that mattered in the world, other than sports and weather, and yet house robbery is rarely mentioned. For the police, it's not a violent crime, so it's a step down from the sort of cases that most detectives tackle. Because of that lack of a spotlight, as well as the enormous riches people have stacked up in their homes in L.A., there are gangs and small teams of thieves pulling the same kind of jobs as us all over town. I wouldn't be surprised to run into one of them one day burglarizing the same house like that scene in the Woody Allen film, *Take the Money and Run*, where the different gangs of bank robbers show up to rob the bank at the same time and argue about whose bank it is to rob."

"In any field, there's always competition," said Dalton.

"I know it's been a long one, but we should meet up tomorrow night to look through this loot and I will make an appointment with one of my regular clients, Harvey Pretzel. Likely, we can bring the stuff to him tomorrow night and return with a wad of cash. It would be grand to go out and celebrate your first job, but of course there is nowhere to get a drink at this time."

"I heard about an after-hours club."

"Would that be worth going to?" questioned Nathan.

"Probably not. I think you have to be 22 and into raves to go to an after-hours club."

"Never been to one. They're kind of an enigma and maybe they should remain that way. I usually stick to diners after the 2 am bar closing time."

"We could go for doughnuts," suggested Dalton.

"Doughnuts would hit the spot. It's cop food, but yummy irresistible cop food."

"Have you ever noticed how there can be three doughnut shops within a couple of blocks in L.A.? How do they remain viable? How does the doughnut dollar spread itself that wide?"

"It's true. I don't believe a doughnut shop has ever closed here. It could be because there are so many pigs," said Nathan, slaphappy.

"So many, damned pigs," added Dalton also sarcastically, but feeling like an outlaw.

~ 8 ~

SLINKY

Smearing an extra dollop of Brylcreem into his stringy, black and gray, greased back hair and then applying a layer of Consort for Men Hair Spray, Harvey Pretzel, the pawn broker, who had six tubes of Brylcreem in the bathroom drawer at his shop, looked into the mirror through his tiny shark-like eyes and smiled a thin, skeletal smile. He applied another dollop to his long, sinewy sideburns to keep them from flaring out, though they were now permanently stuck to the sides of his face. But it was Harvey's metallic gray, flat mustache that was the main feature of his bony face covering nearly a fourth of it like the wings of a hawk; that and his small, square jaw, which opened and closed like a squeaky mailbox.

That skeleton-like head seemed to have been screwed into the wrong body, a much smaller in scale, slightly hunched frame. The rounded shoulders, lack of an ass, and scrawny legs had a reptilian-like quality, which had been commented on by the mean kids of Harvey's youth. It may or may not have contributed to the nickname, Slinky, widely used by his crook friends, as well as others. Harvey didn't mind the nickname at all. He'd been called worse.

Harvey's vintage, Sixties, Van Cort sport shirt was currently in fashion with a much younger set and gave him just a tiny measure of cool, despite being tucked into brown, stained slacks. Harvey was unaware that the old worn shirts in his dresser were coveted by twentysomethings, though Nathan had once complimented him. To complete his everyday attire, Harvey wore beige, beat-up Florsheim loafers, his entire get-up making him appear a bit older than his 56 years.

Keen to leave his pawn shop, Royal Pawn, which was in Cudahy in South L.A., and where no customers had shown up the entire day, and sprint over to the casino at Hollywood Park, the place where he felt perhaps most at home, Harvey gathered his gigantic set of keys and battered leather wallet and set the alarm to the shop.

Stepping into his classic 1960 aquamarine Ford Starliner, the spoils of a high stakes card game, which he had won spectacularly, cheating just a little, he made a right on Atlantic Avenue and then a left on Florence, taking the miserable ghetto thoroughfare through the heart of South Central toward Inglewood's Hollywood Park.

The horse racing track having closed a couple of hours earlier, Harvey headed to the small dingy Hollywood Park Casino next door, passing a man with a bleeding ear. From the outside, lit up at night, the building was to some extent inviting, resembling a genuine casino, but once through the doors, the interior was like a Greyhound Bus station of the damned and drowsily decomposing. Always packed with chirping Chinese men and women, comparatively young Black guys in baseball caps, craggy older ladies, distraught obese couples, cheating invalids, half-sober winos, and career lowlifes of just about every sort, the casino reeked of desperation and small stakes, money being spent and lost at $10 to $50 a pop. At the side of a few of the tables were little roll-up trays of smelly food, sausages and roast beef sandwiches, ordered at the table, so gamblers didn't have to move their immense bodies away from the betting. Despite the small size and wagering of the casino, there was always an impressive amount of security and Harvey knew every security guard. As he entered, he exchanged greetings with Tom and Wilson.

Daryl, the house manager, saw Harvey from across the room and came over to shake hands.

"Good to see ya, boss," said Daryl, looking sharp in a suit, better dressed than anyone in the joint.

"How's the action?" asked Harvey, who spoke in a quiet, toothy manner, the words barely escaping beyond his incisors.

"Busy," replied Daryl, always quick with a tip for Harvey. "You might want to check out Deidre's table, things were popping over there a minute ago."

One of the wealthiest regular patrons of the Hollywood Park Casino, Harvey lived for small-time poker, lifting petty billfolds from insignificant nobodies. Like anybody else, Harvey preferred to win, but had little trouble with losing either. He didn't keep track of his earnings or losses. A gambling addict, he adored the game of poker, as well as other card games, and to a lesser extent betting on the ponies next door, or frankly betting on anything. In some ways, his whole career had been a series of bets, some of which had panned out gloriously, while others had sent him away for protracted stretches.

Among his element at the Hollywood Park Casino, Harvey wasn't the sort to notice or care about the sticky, wormy gambling tables, the gnats flying around the windowless room or the old chips that had gotten stuck together and needed to be pried apart. Aside from all the staff that knew him by name, there were a couple of gambling buddies, which he had met there and made arrangements with. These guys were small-time sharks like him and a quick glance from one of them lead to profits for all. The room was an easy take for a pro who didn't mind the lack of challenge or high rollers. Distracted poker players were always watching the televised horse races, which some of them had bet on, leading to poor decisions and, for Harvey, some extra pocket money. Then, there were the welfare check dunces and the drug dealers high on their own stash, none of whom knew the first thing about gambling and were easy marks at a card table.

After an hour's worth of poker at Deidre's table, in which Harvey had done a little better than breaking even, he noticed English Walter, one of his closest poker shark pals, playing at a nearby table. English Walter, an enormous man with a giant pink pumpkin for a head, who wasn't English at all, gave him the casual smirk that meant there was nothing happening at his table.

"Wanna grab a smoke?" he asked Harvey.

"Sure," said Harvey inaudibly, though he didn't smoke.

They cashed in their chips and stepped outside into the breezy night air, fog setting in over the vast parking lot.

"Heading to Del Mar this weekend. Wanna go?" he asked Harvey, offering him a cigarette.

"No thanks," replied Harvey in a whisper to both the cigarette and the trip, with nothing in the way of an explanation.

English Walter knew Harvey well enough not to expect anything expository from him in the way of words. He liked that quality about him.

"Not feelin' it tonight. Was here earlier in the day. Did okay. I'm $550 up. Hit Commerce earlier, lost 80 bucks or so. Pretty good day. Wanna grab a steak? On me," said English Walter rapid fire.

"Thanks," replied Harvey, "not hungry yet. Doc says I should cut out the red meat."

"Don't they all say that? Who's paying off those quacks, the food pyramid Nazis? I love a good steak. Nothing like cutting into a red, juicy piece of meat and gobbling it down. No doctor's gonna take that away from me. See if they can pry the fork away from my cold, dead hands."

"Ha ha ha," English Walter chortled at his own words.

Harvey grinned, though it wasn't evident. The corners of his mouth half-assed struggled to force a smile. He abhorred people with cameras.

"Know of a poker game on Slauson. Might be worth your while. Lot of colored guys who know their shit. We couldn't pull anything on them, but it's a good game, honest I guess. Won there, lost once. Feel like I got a better handle on the game than some of the other guys in the room. Two of us could play there or you could go on your own and mention English Walter sent you. Would probably be a better idea than us taking money from each other. It's Thursdays at eight-o-clock. Guy has a nice house and provides the brewskis. Name is Jimmy, I think."

"I got a game I go to on Fridays, been going for 15 years," said Harvey. "Been winning for 15 years. Not looking for another private game."

"Suit yourself. Jimmy or whomever runs a good game, a nice mix of punks and pros. Buys some kind of European beer. Daryl told me about it. He's not bad with the cards, knows a trick or two."

"I didn't know he played, but figured maybe," said Harvey.

"Gonna eat me a steak now. Good talkin' to you, Slinky. See you tomorrow?"

"Yeah," replied Harvey, his words like mouse squeaks. "I'll see ya."

Debating whether to go back into the casino again or not, Harvey opted for returning to the pawn shop early before his appointment with Nathan and making himself a fried fish sandwich. The fried fish in the fridge from a couple of days before was likely still edible, he surmised.

Meanwhile, Nathan and Dalton had gone through the loot from the previous night and Nathan had decided to bring the majority of it to Harvey, not the comic book collection, though.

"Can you explain how someone could be named Harvey Pretzel?" asked Dalton as they drove down Alameda, swerving to avoid meteor-sized potholes.

"Not sure, but people actually call him Slinky. I don't know why that is, never asked. And his shop is in Cudahy."

"Where is Cudahy? I have to admit I've never heard of it."

"It's Southeast L.A. You need to expand your horizons. All you know is the Valley. Where is that going to get you in this world?"

Nathan and Dalton pulled behind Royal Pawn past a barbed and razor wire fence and Nathan got out of the car and rang a buzzer. Nathan pulled his Audi into a large two-car garage area attached to the back of the store and filled with junk, Harvey shutting and locking the garage door behind them.

"This is my associate, Dalton Everest," said Nathan.

"Nice to meet ya," whispered Harvey, his handshake so loose that it was like shaking an empty shirt sleeve. "What have we got here?"

Nathan heaved a trash bag full of loot onto a large, industrial steel table and then he and Dalton pulled out several boxes in which they had organized the choicest items. Nathan removed three devices, which he had done some research on and which he knew represented the latest technology, an Apple PowerBook laptop computer, a new, unwrapped DVD player and an Olympus Camedia C-800L digital camera.

With the tiny eyes set back in his skull-like face darting about, Harvey examined each of them without saying a word, turned on the laptop, wrote down the names of the gadgets on a piece of paper and went into the other room to do the same research on his computer.

"$800 for all three," he said unceremoniously upon his return.

"That camera is worth a pretty penny," countered Nathan. "How about $1500?"

Harvey snorted, which was his version of a laugh.

"I can't do much of anything with a used computer, no cord. That's hardly a big ticket item."

"Yeah, but you know that camera is top of the line, latest thing."

"A thousand."

"That'll do," Nathan agreed.

Dalton was admiring a bunch of colorful vintage motorcycle parts Harvey had stacked up in one corner of his garage like a sculpture.

Next, Nathan unrolled a pair of Persian rugs.

"A hundred bucks for the pair," said Harvey barely examining them.

"The blue one is antique and in perfect condition," added Nathan.

"There's nobody banging down my door for Persian rugs," replied Harvey. "That's the best I can do."

"Fine," said Nathan.

Harvey wrote the amounts down on a yellow pad and began to flip through the boxes.

Among the items that Harvey took notice of were a Kenwood turntable, a pair of Cazal sunglasses, a pink Murano glass vase, a silver magnifying glass, a large stack of leather-bound vintage books, a pair of unusual ceramic sculptures, a set of paints, a collection of opera CD sets, and a box full of glittering painted wood frames.

"500 bucks for everything on the table."

"That won't do," replied Nathan. "By itself, that Kenwood turntable is worth $600. Look it up."

Harvey knew turntables from back when he ran a more legitimate pawn shop and was well aware that the turntable was the pick of this lot. He plugged it in, went in the other room, and returned with a Ray Charles record and a pair of speakers, which he frequently used for testing. The sound was crisp.

"Sounds nifty," commented Nathan. "How about $500 for the turntable?"

"It's a nice turntable. I don't think I can get that much for it, though. What would you say to $300 for the turntable and another $300 for the other stuff?"

"I don't know. The designer sunglasses?"

"There's a nick on the side of the glasses, which makes them next to worthless."

"The books are in great shape. Could you do a grand?"

"I could do $700. That's tops."

"Deal."

Dalton wasn't persuaded as to Nathan's bargaining skills, but thought it obvious that Harvey was as accomplished as they come.

Harvey pulled a sizable wad out of his wallet and paid Nathan in hundred dollar bills.

"Thanks as always," said Nathan.

"It's a pleasure," whispered Harvey.

"What do you plan to do with all this stuff?" asked Dalton attempting belatedly to make conversation.

Harvey gave him a look of pronounced disrespect and pity, an eyeballing that was not far removed from his usual expression.

"Sell it," he whispered, his shark eyes pinned on Dalton, as he reopened the garage door.

"That guy had creepiness oozing out of his pores," observed Dalton later on, as Nathan and he had exited the 10 freeway.

"How do you mean?" replied Nathan.

"His hair was so hardened by whatever sort of product he uses. It looked like he could stab you with his sideburns and beyond his resembling some sort of Scooby Doo villain, he had that voice that sounds like the reanimated corpse of a little bird, one that would peck your eyes out, pick them right out of your face like they were pieces of dried fruit."

"I've known Harvey since I was nine years old. He did business with my dad. I believe he started out with a shop on Muscatel Avenue in Rosemead. He's a stand-up character, my best client. The eccentricities go way back. My dad once told me a story about a semi-homeless guy who came into Harvey's pawn shop with this wild energy about him. He claimed to have perfected this water, which was filled with vitamins and minerals and could provide complete nourishment and a total cleanse of the system. So, Harvey was interested for whatever reason and asked the guy to try it first in front of him to make sure it wasn't going to kill him. Then both he and an employee tried it. Later in the day, the employee admitted that he had just pretended to drink it, but Harvey had drunk as much as a cup. After twenty minutes or so, Harvey started hallucinating and lost all of his marbles. According to my dad, Harvey was never the same after that."

"That dude is a creep, not a client."

"He's never done wrong by me," said Nathan, paused at a stoplight downtown, pulling $600 out of his wallet and handing it to Dalton.

~ 9 ~

FROGTOWN

Upon entering the 99 Cents Only Store on Sunset Boulevard in Silver Lake, LAPD Detective Orlando Talbert, massaging his thick mustache in consternation, was keenly aware that his police career was not taking off on the trajectory he had once hoped for. Once, on his lunch break, he had shopped at this store, and had been astonished to find some real pearls among the muck. This time, on a robbery investigation, he felt like just another customer (though the only Black one) on a doomed shopping spree marked only by its cheap irrelevance. After nine years on the force, the gripping homicide case that should be the apex of any police detective's life's work was as distant as it had ever been. As usual, he was chasing down some lowlife punk, who was sticking up convenience stores, taco stands, and auto part shops across the Eastside, an all too familiar trail that would surely end with Detective Talbert or another officer apprehending the suspect, who was careless and desperate.

At the checkout stand where there were three people in line, Talbert, in a voice deep and impassive, asked the tiny Latina lady scanning items, "Is there a Barbara here?"

"Barbara's over there," she said, pointing to a younger Latina lady at the other checkout line.

Barbara was also scanning items and Talbert didn't see any reason to interrupt her work, as he just needed her to look at a photo.

"Barbara, Detective Talbert, LAPD."

He pulled out his badge.

"The guy that robbed the place, was it this guy?"

Talbert pulled out a tiny black and white photo shot at a side angle from a security camera of a young Latino with short hair and narrow eyes. For a security camera still, it was a clear shot of the culprit.

Still scanning items, Barbara took a good look at the photo.

"I think that's him," she said.

"You're sure?" asked Talbert.

"Yes."

"Is the manager Horace around?"

"Horace!" she yelled.

A portly, bespectacled man with a perfectly round head, Horace, hobbled over clutching a pack of some very reasonably priced 1-ply toilet paper in his hands.

"Hello, I'm Detective Talbert. Is this the man that robbed the place?"

Horace released the toilet paper, took the photo in his swollen hands and carefully examined it.

"I believe that's him. You got him quick. I told the uniformed cops, he's a real nervous one, a little weird I would say. He grabbed some chewing gum and some chocolate bars and put them in a bag, while Barbara was emptying the cash register. This guy, he also kept asking for cigarettes, but we don't sell cigarettes. And he was pointing that huge gun at everyone."

"He hasn't been arrested yet," said Talbert. "You're sure it was the man in the photo?"

"Yes, positive. That's him," replied Horace pointing at the photo. "I hope you find him soon. He's a menace. And anything I can do to help, I will."

"Thanks," said Talbert, curtly, as he left the store.

"What type of horse dooky is this?" he considered, as he entered his unmarked Chevy Lumina slamming the door. "Always talking to these morons, always stuck with cases anyone with two brain cells could solve. Why? 'Cause the criminals are bubble gum thieves, that's why! If their mommas would have just given them a proper hiding once in a while, these brats would have turned out okay and ended up with real jobs."

Fed up with the day already, Talbert decided to grab an early lunch and knew there was a Fatburger, a somewhat beloved local takeout chain, nearby on Vermont Avenue. He managed to kill an hour and a half there flipping through the file of this case, the only one he had currently, which he considered beneath his investigative prowess.

Back in the car, he called Jorge, his number one local source of information who reported only to him in exchange for the mildest of LAPD favors such as a lackadaisical parole agent.

"Jorge, I'm coming over. I've got a picture I need you to look at," insisted Talbert.

Arriving at Manitou Avenue in Lincoln Heights, Talbert parked in front of Jorge's sullen apartment building. Walking up to the second floor, he knocked and Jorge opened the door.

"Hey," said Jorge unenthusiastically, letting Detective Talbert in.

Talbert pulled out the same picture of the 99 Cents Only Store robber.

"You know this guy?" he asked.

Jorge studied the photograph.

"Yeah, that's Jesus. I know him from county. He's from around here somewheres. Everyone knows Jesus. He's stupid. I don't think he runs with any gangs. He's just like ... your average criminal, I don't know."

"Last name?"

"Rojas. I'm positive, yeah, Rojas."

"That's all I need. I'll be seeing ya," said Talbert, a little impressed with himself for getting a suspect ID'd after being on the case for half a day, most of which he had spent dillydallying at Fatburger.

With that, the issue on Talbert's mind was whether he was going to immediately let every cop on the force know about Jesus Rojas, clearly the protocol, or wait until late afternoon or evening to do that if he was unsuccessful in catching Rojas himself by day's end. And really, for a detective who was a minority in a rigged and racist organization with scattered white supremacists throughout, the only way to go was to take advantage of any opportunity he might find to stand out as commendable. This was a legitimate challenge, and the tiny nugget of information that gave him encouragement was that Rojas was from the immediate area, something he had suspected anyways by the pattern of robberies.

"I can catch this turkey today, probably in the act," he said in a motivational speech to himself. "I'm practically staring his dumb ass down already."

He called the DMV (Department of Motor Vehicles) and Jesus Rojas came up, clearly the same one, who drove a light blue Toyota Tercel hatchback and whose car registration had expired. There was an address and a license plate number, too. Rojas' last registered address was on Blimp Street in a neighborhood colloquially known as Frogtown, next to the L.A. River. Talbert drove straight over.

The tiny brown shack was a little intimidating with a barking bulldog chained up in front. Talbert gave it a thorough examination from his car window, but the barking dog caused him to park at the end of the street pondering his next move.

The place looked lifeless and there was no car parked nearby. A Black man, Talbert would stand out sitting in a car in Frogtown, a mostly Latino neighborhood. But if Jesus still called the shack home, it was unlikely he had neighbors or family nearby that would first notice Talbert sitting there and then somehow warn Jesus to stay clear. This was as good as it was going to get. He needed no further clues. If he got restless, he could question the neighbors. But the best course of action was unmistakably to sit tight.

And he did so for three and a half hours, quietly tuning into his police radio and then turning on his regular radio and switching between R&B, oldies, and AM sports talk and news.

"Dodgers suck it so bad," he chuckled to himself.

As the sun started to dip to the west, he called his wife, Marie, a registered nurse, who was about to leave the clinic.

"Honey, I could be out all night. I have no idea," he said.

"Okay, well, I guess I will see you when I see you," replied Marie.

"Might get home tonight, maybe late, really don't know," he repeated.

"Okay then."

"Bye bye."

From television shows and such, Talbert was pretty sure the policeman's wife was supposed to worry about her husband. That had not really been the case in the year and a half of marriage he had with Marie. His ex-wife had fretted more about his police work. Marie seemed to only worry about money: the mortgage payments on their West Adams home, spending too much on groceries, and utter bullshit like that, he considered. It's not that he required a wife that was constantly apprehensive about being married to a cop. Those kinds of wives were really no use. Marie rarely asked him questions about his work, which was fine because he didn't want to talk to her about it anyways. But she didn't even seem curious; it was as if he sold insurance or fixed roofs.

"Whatever," he thought, "as long as she isn't running around like that tramp I used to be married to."

A couple of men had come home from work and parked on the street, and none of them were immediate neighbors of the house in question. Finally, at 6:45, a Latino man walked up the street and entered the house. Talbert got a decent look at him and it was not Jesus Rojas. However, it could easily have been a relative or friend. It was time to make a move, he decided. The dog, though, looked like it would be a pain in the ass.

Talbert pulled his lengthy and muscular frame out of the car and walked the full span of the block, well aware that he looked like a cop or a parole officer in his brown suit to anyone that might catch a glimpse of him. The bulldog started up two houses down, barking and growling ferociously. Talbert opened the three-foot-high chain link gate attached to the fence that surrounded the shack, observing that the dog would not be able to reach him from where it was tethered.

He knocked the hard police style knock on the flimsy door, shouting, "LAPD, open up!"

Nothing.

"Open up!" he shouted, pounding on the door again.

"Okay, coming," he heard from inside.

The man, a short squat fellow with a receding hairline, who he had seen walk into the house opened and peeked out of the door.

"What do you need?" he asked meekly.

"Is Jesus Rojas here?" Talbert asked.

"No," he replied defensively.

"Anyone else in the house?"

"Nobody."

"Let me see some ID," demanded Talbert.

"Aw, shit. I'll go get it," said the man, attempting to close the door before doing so.

Talbert caught the door and swung it open.

"You got a warrant?" asked the man.

Knowing he was straddling the line between a circumstance where he may or may not need a warrant, Talbert peered into the living room of the shack. Sitting on a glass table were at least twenty packs of unopened cigarettes, different brands. It was enough evidence for him. He remembered what the idiot at the 99 Cents Only Store had said about Rojas asking for cigarettes. No one smoked a variety of cigarette brands and left twenty packs lying out on a living room table, except perhaps the lowliest of thieves.

He grabbed the man firmly by the arm, pulling it behind the man's back and yanked out his cuffs. Meeting little resistance, he could tell by the way the man fell into the position of someone being cuffed that the man had been through this routine before.

"Where'd you steal those cigarettes from?"

"Those aren't mine."

"Really. Where's that ID of yours?"

"In the other room."

Talbert marched the cuffed man in front of him toward the other room.

The man sighed as he nudged the door open with his head.

Inside the tiny, disheveled bedroom, there were several piles of cash, unimpressive amounts, laid out on one bed. Talbert looked through a couple of heaps of small bills. It looked like maybe a thousand bucks or perhaps two, hardly drug dealer piles.

"Where's the ID?" Talbert asked again.

"In that drawer," said the suspect indicating with his head.

Talbert opened the drawer and pulled out the ID. The suspect's name was Gabriel Rojas.

Looking over Gabriel Rojas, who had his head down in the position of a repentant criminal, Talbert asked, "You're Jesus' brother?"

"Yeah."

"Where is Jesus?"

"I don't know."

"It's better you tell me. You don't want your brother getting shot down. It would be preferable to have him in jail rather than dead, right?"

"I don't know where he is," repeated Gabriel flustered.

Pulling out his cell phone, Talbert called in the arrest, requesting that the officers come in plain clothes with an unmarked car in case Jesus returned, so as not to scare him off. The officer on the line got a hold of Gabriel Rojas' record, which was extensive, grand theft and the like, though he had surprisingly been out of the clink and squeaky clean for eight years.

Around the tiny hovel, there was evidence of penny-ante thievery: unopened packages of cigarettes, alcohol, candy, and chewing gum.

Talbert read Gabriel Rojas his Miranda rights.

"Where are the guns?" Talbert asked.

"No guns," replied Gabriel.

"Look, we have your brother on camera armed and robbing a quickie mart. Where the guns at?"

"I don't know nothing about no guns," said Gabriel.

It took nearly a half hour for two officers to arrive. Officer Gomez was the most well liked and friendliest officer in Northwest Division and so had been partnered with a rookie, Officer Bradley, an oversized marine looking youngster with a permanent glower for a face.

The three officers bagged all the evidence and then let Officer Bradley take it back to the division, along with Gabriel

Rojas to be held and interrogated later. Presently, Talbert and Gomez would stake out the house from the inside awaiting Jesus Rojas' return. Gomez grabbed a shotgun from the unmarked squad car. They called L.A. Animal Services to come and take the bulldog away, which had been barking and growling nonstop.

"I'd expect that if he comes back here, he'll be armed," said Talbert. "Fo' sure, he's a dummy, so take that any way you like."

"Man, he's just another stupid kid," added Gomez smiling and sitting on a chair at a right angle from the front door armed with a shotgun.

"If he actually shows, we'll have the jump on him," said Talbert, peering out the window behind a curtain.

"You think he'll show?" asked Gomez.

"If he hasn't gotten wind of his brother getting rousted, I think he will stumble back here."

But another glacial two and half hours passed and Talbert and Gomez had run through all of the department gossip they could scrounge up. They had drunk from a perhaps stolen, unopened bottle of RC Cola, which they had found in the kitchen and had joked about ordering a pizza. L.A. Animal Services came by, tranquilized the bulldog and tossed it into the back of their truck. Eventually, Talbert and Gomez had run out of subjects they were mutually interested in and an impatient silence settled over the dark, gloomy living room of the shack.

"I'm going to call the division and get some other fools to stake out this roach trap," said Talbert. "You've done your time. Feel free to call it a day."

"I can stick around until they arrive. I don't want to leave you here by yourself," said Gomez sincerely.

"No, I got it," replied Talbert. "Thanks for everything."

Gomez walked back to his unmarked car, for the second time revealing the shotgun to any neighbors who might have been curious, and drove away.

Talbert peered out the window every few minutes until the replacement car pulled up. Officer McNeil and a blonde, buff female cop, Officer Anderson, were strangers to Talbert. He filled them in on the basics of the case, handed them the photo of Jesus Rojas and suggested they move their car away from the front of the house. After moving the car, Officer Anderson then sauntered down the block while holding a shotgun, just in case there was anyone left in the neighborhood unaware that something was up.

Talbert returned to his car and drank a few sips from a cup of cold, disgusting coffee that had been left in his car from the morning. It was 11:30 pm. He could let Gabriel Rojas sit for the night and interrogate him in the morning. It looked like he had him on aiding and abetting, possession of stolen property, and not much more unless a witness could place him at a robbery. All the robbery reports mentioned one perp, but one of them could have been Gabriel Rojas. However, Talbert figured Jesus was the stickup man and Gabriel perhaps held a real job and had just been a fool to let his younger brother run around robbing everyone within 20 miles, and to then leave stacks of stolen money and junk all over the house. Likely, they were both sharing the paltry spoils.

He made a U-turn, drove past the shack, then made a right, and as he turned, he passed a light blue Toyota Tercel hatchback. Both cars were traveling slowly under a street lamp and Jesus Rojas and Talbert got a good long look at each other, the recognition on Talbert's face leading to alarm on Jesus Rojas' face. Knowing he had been made as a cop, Talbert swung his Chevy Lumina around wildly with a cop car screech to the tires, as Jesus took off gaining more than a block on him.

Barreling along Blake Avenue through quiet, residential Frogtown, Jesus pulled a hard left on Coolidge and then an immediate right on Ripple Street in an attempt to not be penned in by the neighborhood, which had the L.A. River on one side and the 5 freeway looming on the other. But his old Tercel didn't have any kick to it at all and Talbert was almost immediately on top of him. He placed his siren on top of his car and stayed glued to Jesus' bumper. Having been in a few car chases, Talbert chuckled at Jesus' sputtering Tercel, knowing he'd nabbed him. But it was policy that he had to call in a car chase, even one going 45 miles per hour, and so he did. Finally, turning on Fletcher Drive and heading unknowingly in the direction of the LAPD's Northeast Division, Jesus heard other police sirens and could feel impending doom settling upon him, as he slowed down and Talbert pulled up next to him.

"Pull over Jesus, or I'll turn you and your little shitmobile into a pile of scrap," he yelled.

Jesus gave in and hit the brakes.

Talbert pulled up to his bumper.

"Jesus, get the fuck out the car, but slow-like, keeping your hands away from your body, and then place them on top of the car!"

Jesus, dressed in a blue sweatshirt and looking dead to the world, got out of the car and did as instructed.

Talbert came up on him, pistol drawn, then holstered it, cuffed Jesus and patted him down.

"Where's the gun at, Jesus?"

No response.

Inside the hatchback, Talbert plainly spotted a 99 Cents Only Store bag, along with a lot of the same junk, cigarettes and candy bars, as had been seen in the shack.

"Been shopping at the 99 Cents Store recently, Jesus? They got some good deals there. I noticed you can get three Mars Bars for 99 cents. You don't have to steal that. If you got yourself a job, even the shittiest job in the world, you can afford that kind of junk. Everyone's a millionaire at the 99 Cents Store. Not you, though, you a dumb-ass."

As three squad cars pulled up, Talbert had sat Jesus down on the curb in front of the long dormant and perhaps now out of place Van De Kamp's Bakery Building, which had red tiled roofs in the style of a sixteenth-century Dutch townhouse. Positive that Jesus wouldn't try and scamper away cuffed, Talbert reached under the passenger's seat of the Tercel and discovered Jesus' .44 Magnum.

He could scarcely believe his good luck. It was his collar, and he had just begun looking into the case that very morning.

Handing Jesus over to some uniformed officers for the short drive back to Northwest Division, Talbert began gloating to himself, over what another detective might conclude was hardly a major arrest.

"Racist shit-for-brains lieutenants can't keep me down. I got more cop in me than all y'all put together! Who's your next homicide investigator? Me, you Nazi fucks, me!" he thought to himself in a revelry of self-congratulation.

Jesus' bashed Tercel was spilling over with stolen junk requiring the use of every evidence bag they could find in three squad cars. The Tercel itself, with all its doors and its hatchback opened, seemed to be weeping.

Back at Northwest Division, a dilapidated police station that sat on San Fernando Road in Glassell Park in a commercial area of cheap, crummy stores that many officers referred to as "Crap Central," Detective Talbert bumped into McNeil and Anderson, whom he had just met an hour earlier. They both congratulated him on the collar, but that was all the praise he would get at that late hour in the mostly deserted police station. Both Jesus and Gabriel Rojas were locked up in separate cells, as he had requested. He walked to the office where his desk was, for no particular reason, or perhaps hoping he might come upon someone whom he knew and could share his victory with, but no one was around at that hour.

~ 10 ~

NATHAN HOPS A FENCE

In the days following his first burglary, Dalton resumed his previous life for the most part, but not quite. Having done very well at a comic book store with the stolen collection, Nathan called him to tell him that he would be floating him another $700 of the $2500 he had scored. For some time, Dalton had been putting off the plans he usually made to meet up with his high school chums, but finally agreed to meet the group at Capri Lounge, a tiny bar with a house jazz quartet led by the owner of the bar, saxophonist Jimmie Maddin. This obscure wonder of a jazz dive located on Pacific Avenue just up the street from another bar, Sidebar, in Glendale, but otherwise not near anything of note, was actually a discovery of Nathan's. Having never been there, Dalton knew it was strange to suggest that he and his friends meet there and not invite Nathan, not that Nathan would necessarily want to come. But Dalton had concluded that he must keep his friendship with Nathan and their criminal enterprise entirely separate from his old friends, his teaching, and the very ordinary life he had once led. Otherwise, he feared everything might come crashing down upon him.

Arriving at Capri Lounge ambivalent on the subject of what to talk about with his closest friends, Dalton felt reassured in every way upon seeing Leah, Patrick, and Dudley seated at a small table. There were just a few other people in the bar. As Dalton joined them, Jimmie Maddin, the bar's elderly proprietor, dressed in a pin-striped zoot suit and strangely sporting fingerless gloves, came up to their table to greet them.

"Thanks for stopping by," he said warmly. "Very nice to meet you. In a little while, my band is going to play a swingin' set. I've played with Dizzy Gillespie, Duke Ellington, Benny Carter, anyone you can name. I used to have my own TV show, Jimmie Maddin Show. You all, please enjoy yourselves. Stay tuned."

The group was excited about the entertainment, despite the deserted bar.

"So, where's Nathan?" asked Leah. "Is he coming?"

Dalton couldn't believe that was the first thing he was asked.

"I haven't seen him much," replied Dalton.

"First, that French tart ditches you and then Nathan, who introduced her to you, also disappears. Did they run off together? Why don't you ever call me anymore? Are you suffering?" she asked half sarcastically, half concerned.

"I'm fine," said Dalton. "I don't think they ran off together."

"That's it?" chimed in Dudley. "Leah said you were sort of dating this French girl?"

"No, we weren't dating. What can I say? She wasn't into me, story of my life, not the type of girl I'd bring home to meet mom, anyways."

"I don't mean to drag your dirty laundry into the harsh public light," said Leah, "but you were crazy about this girl, right? You can talk to us. You've known us since we were wearing ugly olive green P.E. shorts together and running around a track in some sort of forced labor camp called junior high school."

"I liked her a lot, but I'm a big enough adult to realize when a girl is out of my league and that was most definitely the case. Melanee liked to be chauffeured around. She guzzled liquor like I used to drink Yoohoo on a hot summer day. Then, she sobered up and like that, I was yesterday's guacamole."

"I'm sorry man," said Patrick. "I don't know about Leah, who is just a gossip. But the rest of us here are your homies and we care about you. Don't be a stranger. My girlfriend broke up with me last year and it was rough going."

"Didn't she break up with you because she found out you love roly-poly, red-cheeked men?" asked Leah.

"That might have had something to do with it," said Patrick, faux downcast.

"But weren't you and Nathan drinking buddies?" Leah asked, turning her attention back to Dalton. "Are you saying that big hunk just flew the coop too?"

"No, I saw him a while back. I don't know if you're his type. He told me he doesn't like girls who smell like old bookstores."

"I think you are being kind of evasive, just like you said he was," retorted Leah. "Did you ever decipher the mystery of what he did for a living?"

"I asked him about that," revealed Dudley hesitantly. "That dude is a piece of work. He fuckin' assaulted me."

"What do you mean, he assaulted you?" asked Leah.

"He grabbed me by the balls and threatened me," explained Dudley.

"How is that possible?" questioned Patrick stunned, as all of them were.

"It's just like I said. I asked him some questions about what sort of post-production work he had done. He became mortally offended, literally grabbed me by the balls and told me he'd rip them off if I asked him any more questions."

"I'm glad you're not friends with that prick anymore," added Dudley to Dalton.

"That's not normal behavior," exclaimed Leah.

"Where did he do this?" asked Patrick.

"That time when we were at the Formosa," replied Dudley.

"Didn't you say at the time that you never asked him about his job?" questioned Leah.

"I was scared of that prick. You don't expect that sort of reaction when you ask someone about their work. What else do people normally talk about in L.A.?"

At first, there had been a little bit of disbelief among the group of friends, but with only a few words of explanation, everyone was in Dudley's corner.

"Again, Dalton, you haven't said one friggin' thing? What is up with this guy?" asked Leah interrogating Dalton.

"I ... don't know. I haven't seen him. He's not like us. I don't know what to say."

This response struck the rest of them to be as out of left field as Dudley's story.

"Dude, what's happened to you?" asked Dudley disturbed. "What did this prick do to you?"

Dalton's brow became heavy with perspiration. He hadn't prepared himself to be grilled. There wasn't a plausible story that he could conjure up on the spot. Really, he wanted to tell them about Harvey Pretzel and his pawn shop in Cudahy and stealing a car and being handed a wad of bills for burglarizing a house. But there was no way he was going to do that.

"I met him at the Roost. We both shared this sincere appreciation of L.A.'s old bars and art deco architecture and such. Not at any time did I figure him to be a ball grabber. Obviously, I have no explanation for that."

Dalton felt he had finally succeeded in being at least somewhat convincing of his non-culpability. He felt he was a little older and plenty wiser since he had last seen his friends.

"My crush has evaporated," said Leah. "This guy is a real fucko."

Some older gentlemen, who had been gathered in the corner of the bar near the door where there was a drum set, pulled out their instruments and launched into a tune with no introduction. There was a keyboardist, a drummer, a trombonist, and Jimmie Maddin leading the band with a tenor sax and a charming, rickety voice. They did a set of mostly upbeat standards and a couple of rollicking originals, penned by Maddin, pausing after each song to debate the next one they would play.

The group felt superlatively fortunate to have stumbled into such groovy, free entertainment performing for them and the two other lone souls in the room.

"I started a tab at the bar," said Dudley, as they got up to leave.

"I've got it," said Dalton.

"What?" asked Patrick surprised.

"I've got the bill," repeated Dalton.

"Since when do you offer to pay for everyone's drinks?" asked Leah.

"I've handled the check before," replied Dalton.

"Um, maybe a round," said Patrick. "In my memory, you have never offered to pick up an entire bill before."

"Now, you are acting like Nathan," said Leah, somewhat suspicious, but otherwise just being herself. "Are you on drugs? Did he get you into some sort of narcotics?"

"Yes," replied Dalton. "I'm paying the bill because I am in the cocaine trade now and all this money is just burning a hole in my pocket."

This sarcasm was a not so distant cousin of the truth.

After batting it around for a couple of days, Dalton came to the realization that he didn't much care about the incident at the Formosa, but thought that perhaps Nathan had possessed some justification for attacking Dudley. In any case, Dudley could be obnoxious, and Dalton had not exactly condoned Leah's suggestion to harass Nathan about his work. By no means, he concluded, while sitting at a stop light at Sunset and Chautauqua Boulevard in the Pacific Palisades in a stolen Honda Odyssey minivan, was he going to bother Nathan about this unfortunate incident of the distant past.

Zoning out into a tangle of inconsequential thoughts, Dalton was abruptly startled by repeated flashing high beams from the vehicle behind him.

"Holy mackerel!" exclaimed Dalton. "Should I pull over?"

"It's just some wise ass who can't be bothered to change lanes," answered Nathan.

Dalton rolled down his window as the Mercedes passed him.

"Don't flip him the bird," commanded Nathan. "We can do without the attention."

Pulling in front of the tasteless pillared mansion of a successful TV producer, they parked the minivan at the curb, Nathan scanning the street and grabbing his bag of tools.

"This place might be loaded. If that's the case, I may need you to come in and help me," said Nathan, who then bolted from the car.

In one quick motion, Nathan was over the fence and away from the prying eyes of insomnia-suffering neighbors. He was familiar with the alarm monitoring company advertised on the security lawn sign and quickly located the power line and cut it, knocking out the alarm. Then, he went to work on the lock and was in the back door in less than a minute. Switching on a flashlight, he looked around the gleaming kitchen loaded with the latest and most expensive appliances. It was rare that anyone kept anything valuable in kitchens of the sort Nathan could remove and make a profit on. If he felt at ease in a house, regarding how much time he had, he might hit the kitchen last and grab a fancy knife set, a bottle of imported wine or a high end espresso machine.

He moved into the next room, but there was a distant light source and Nathan pondered it, bewildered for a moment. The light grew larger and met the light from his flashlight. Then it hit him: the light source coming tentatively nearer, the nearly silent footsteps. A person was approaching and then they were right in front of him.

"Can you switch back on the lights? Did I leave the back door open?"

The voice was unthreatening, a girl, youthful, not quite awake.

Nathan wasn't sure what to say. He gulped a couple of breaths. Her light hit his face as he, in turn, aimed his flashlight at her.

He gulped another couple of breaths.

"Who are you? Can you fix the lights? I can show you where the breakers are."

It made no sense, what she was saying.

She had curly, long brown hair, darkish skin, half-closed eyes, and a light blue nightgown.

"Where are the breakers, ma'am?" he asked.

"Follow me," she said, her voice still relaxed, friendly, almost delicate, a little bit dreamy.

He followed her back through the kitchen into a laundry room.

She pointed her flashlight at the electrical panel.

"There," she said.

He switched all the breakers off and on.

"It could be an issue with the outside wiring. You go back to sleep. I should have the power back up in an hour or so. I won't bother you again. I'll let myself out and lock the door."

"Don't go. It's so dark in here," she said embracing him. It was a light squeeze, her fingertips on his back, her face against his chest.

Nathan's body tingled at her touch. He smelled her hair. He lost himself.

She raised her head, and in the moonlight from a high window, he looked into her sleepy, green eyes. He couldn't see her body at all, but it was up against his and plainly being offered to him.

"Hey, Mr. Electrical Man," she said, "you've already flipped my switch."

He kissed her and she gently pushed his mouth away, took his large, bear-like paw and placed it at the lower part of her nightgown.

"That's the spot," she said in full-tilt horny mode with a little deepness to her voice now. "That will get the power back on."

Her fingertips again were touching him now lightly at waist level.

"Hey big guy," she said, "Why don't you go get a condom?"

Nathan didn't know what to make of anything. He had lost all control.

"Where?" he asked.

She pointed her flashlight through the kitchen.

"Just past that door, then on the right and through another door to the garage. They're on the shelf in a brown wooden box at the bottom," she said killing the mood a little.

"You keep your condoms in the garage?" he asked.

"It would be ruinous if my dad found them. He's an asshole. This is his house. I don't live here, thank God."

She patted him on his rear.

"Go get them, sweetie. I will meet you in my bedroom. We'll keep the lights off."

Finding his way to the garage, Nathan for the first time questioned the odd happenings that had befallen him. He was in a strange garage rummaging around for condoms to have sex with the daughter of the person whose house he was robbing and he had yet to see her under sufficient lighting.

As he feverishly searched for the wooden box containing the condoms, there was a sudden noise behind him. He turned around with his flashlight just in time to catch a glimpse of the girl's curly dark hair and the door closing behind her, clearly locked. Nathan went straight for the door, but then realized he had left his bag with his tools somewhere in the house. His cell phone was with it. As he scanned the room with his flashlight for the garage door switch, it occurred to him that of course he had killed the power, and a pull cord, which would open the garage door manually, wasn't where it should be.

He heard a distant voice through the door, the girl was on the phone, but he had also cut the phone wires. It had to be her own cell phone and her tone of voice was distinctly dissimilar from how it was previously, no surprise to him now. He knew he had been a spectacular fool and hers had been a stellar performance. But he was sure she was speaking with someone familiar to her, likely not the police and that made little sense to him.

The bolt lock on the door to the kitchen wasn't a simple one. He would need actual tools, a wire or a screwdriver wasn't going to do it. It was clear to Nathan that his situation was dire, so he decided he would try to break down the door, which looked sturdy. Leaning his shoulder into it and using the full weight of his nearly 200-pound frame, he slammed himself against the door, but it barely budged. The girl screamed.

Outside, Dalton was feeling conspicuous parked in the minivan. A few cars had passed by. A dog barked. He had not heard the girl's scream. Again, he found himself hungry at this ungodly hour of the night and contemplated the few burger stands and doughnut shops that he knew were open all night in Hollywood and the Valley, though they were distant from the far Westside. Time was proceeding at a sluggish pace.

Pulling directly in front of him, a car appeared, backed up and parked. There was no time to duck out of view. A boy got out of the car hurriedly. He was tallish and skinny with a mess of brown hair that looked like a shaggy bathroom mat. It appeared he had not noticed Dalton sitting in plain view in the minivan behind him. The boy pressed a buzzer on the gate of the house several times. Then moving a bit closer to the minivan, but still not observing Dalton, the boy quickly scaled the fence.

Dalton grabbed his cell phone and called Nathan, but it rang continuously with no response.

"If that kid was trying to buzz his way through the gate, there must be someone else in the house," thought Dalton, still a little mystified.

Too much time had passed, though Dalton had no idea how long he had been sitting there.

He got out of the minivan.

"Here goes nothing," he whispered aloud to himself as he struggled to pull himself over the fence. It took him nearly a minute.

As he scampered, not so stealthily across the front yard, Dalton heard what sounded like someone rummaging around in the garage and spotted a faint light beneath the garage door. He decided it was more likely to be Nathan than whomever was in the house.

"Nathan, is that you?" Dalton whispered.

"Yes," Nathan responded immediately. "I am locked in here. You'll need to get in through the back of the house. The door to the garage is straight through the kitchen and then on your right. There is a girl and her boyfriend in the house. I think they are calling the police, so hurry your ass!"

"Got it," replied Dalton.

Dalton quickly came around the back of the house. There was just enough moonlight to see through the French doors, which were slightly ajar, and there in the kitchen he saw the boy again. The boy was sitting up against the kitchen counter looking in the opposite direction. Dalton did not see the girl.

Quietly opening the French doors, Dalton lunged at the boy and cold-cocked him on the ear. The punch was a tremendous one and sent the boy flying like a lifeless doll, crashing against the oven door and finally collapsing onto the kitchen tile barely conscious. Following Dalton's instructions, he found the garage door in the pitch dark and unlocked it. Nathan emerged.

"Let's scram," he whispered.

They moved quickly through the kitchen.

"Good work," he whispered seeing the boy sprawled on the floor.

"One second," Nathan said pausing at the door.

He went into the next room to retrieve his tool bag. But while bending down to find it in the dark, a faint light came rushing toward them. Nathan was so intent on finding his bag that he didn't react for the second time, while Dalton didn't know what to make of it. As he grabbed his bag, the girl emerged with her flashlight in one hand and an Emmy Award in the other. Brandishing the sharp wings of the statuette as a weapon, she slashed at Nathan's face. Putting his arm out to protect himself, Nathan yelled as one of the wings went straight into his left forearm. With his other arm, he ripped the award away from the girl, considered for a second the option of smiting her with it as she screamed like Carrie and then tossed the award against the wall. Nathan and Dalton then scurried out the door, both turning back to keep their eyes on the girl, who was screaming in the darkness, behind them.

As they ran around the side of the house, the girl followed them outside, then stopped, and Nathan, still keeping his eyes on the girl, caught a good glimpse of her in the moonlight.

"She was not much of a looker," he thought.

This time, both Nathan and Dalton flew swiftly over the fence and into the minivan.

There were lights on at the house next door and standing in front of the house was a neighbor, a man in red and white striped pajamas, who got a decent look at them.

Dalton fumbled getting the minivan started. The man approached slightly, though he hardly looked menacing. Dalton got the engine going and they burned rubber getting out of there. In the distance, there was the distinct sound of police sirens. The sound put a chill in Dalton's heart.

"Okay. Drive normal, a little fast, but normal, not like you're escaping a crime scene," instructed Nathan. "Take Chautauqua south to the beach, then make a hard left onto Channel Road just as you hit the beach."

Nathan opened his window to check which direction the sirens were coming from, as Dalton drove the minivan up Channel Road and past San Vicente Boulevard.

"Pull down any side street. We are going to ditch the car here," said Nathan with some strain in his voice.

Blood was dripping from his sleeve.

"But then what are we going to do?" sputtered Dalton, panicked.

"We'll have to play that by ear."

Dalton stopped the car on a residential street. No one was around at 4 am. They got out and walked briskly.

"It would be best if we split up," said Nathan, as distant sirens still wailed. "I have to hide these tools somewhere and figure out what to do about this hole in my arm. I'd get rid of that sweater that you are wearing, just throw it in a trashcan somewhere, and make sure no one sees you do that."

"I love this sweater," said Dalton in all seriousness.

"If I were you, I would toss it. That stripe is about the only thing identifiable about you from a distance. Walk down one of these residential streets until you hit Wilshire. Look for a taxi there. You probably won't find one. More likely, look for a phone booth and call a taxi, but have them pick you up on a side street, not on Wilshire. Do not wait out in the open for the taxi. If the driver asks you any questions, make up a story. You are leaving your girlfriend's place or something, whatever. We're particularly noticeable because there aren't so many people around at this hour, so the quicker we get out of here, the better. If you see a bus, get on it and see where it takes you."

"Okay. I'll do it. What are you going to do about your arm?"

In this tense moment of escape and pursuit, Nathan appreciated Dalton's concern for his well-being. He knew he had done well to choose him as an accomplice.

"I don't think it's that serious. Tomorrow I will go see a doctor. I'm going to head in a different direction and look for a taxi," he said while wrapping his leather belt around his bloody arm.

"Thanks for your heroic exploits this evening," he continued. "I'll talk to you later when we both get back. Make haste."

The whole screwy evening had unfolded so rapidly that Dalton was just now wondering how Nathan had ended up locked in a garage, as he walked down pleasant, residential 7th Street on a cool, foggy morning past several belligerent "don't let your dog poop on my lawn" signs.

At Wilshire Boulevard, he encountered a tall and lanky fellow with poorly bleached blonde hair wearing jeans and sporting a full midriff. The man pulled something out of his hair and flicked it, grumbling "motherfucker."

Dalton then headed east on Wilshire spotting neither a taxi, nor a phone booth. On his way, he passed a grandma going for a morning walk in brown velveteen exercise pants, an adult woman on a kid's bike, clearly riding to work, and a man with Rodney Bingenheimer hair, perhaps homeless, wearing a Sgt. Pepper's looking outfit crossing the intersection of Wilshire and Euclid diagonally.

Eventually, he noticed a phone booth on the other side of the street and crossed. The noise of the police sirens had stopped, but upon reaching the opposite curb, a cop car passed just behind him. The cop in the passenger's seat, wearing sunglasses despite the lack of sun, looked directly at Dalton and he looked right back at him, fixated in the moment of his conceivable downfall. He had previously dumped the striped sweater into a trashcan. For a second there, it seemed like it was time to roll the credits. But the cop car did not slow down. Dalton called a taxi and made it back to his loft safe and sound. And the exhilarating feeling that Nathan had described at the outset of his career in crime, well that was exactly how he felt reliving the moment when he had punched that boy and sprung Nathan from the garage.

That morning, Nathan also made it back to his duplex smoothly, but during the taxi ride, he caught the driver looking at his bleeding arm in the rear view mirror and thought it prudent to offer him $600 to keep quiet. The taxi driver was exceedingly keen on the dough and thanked Nathan effusively.

A few hours later, Nathan woke up with the room spinning and sharp pangs of pain springing from the wound. It had been a long time since he had called Dr. Wendell Foxhide, another former associate of his father, and he hadn't missed calling Dr. Foxhide any, but this seemed like the moment to make the call.

"Dr. Foxhide, Nathan Lyme," he said into the receiver.

"Nathan, it's good to hear from you. You're okay?" asked Dr. Foxhide, who appeared to have been roused from sleep.

"Actually, I have something I need you to look at rather urgently. Are you free this morning?"

"Yes, toot toot toot. It would be no problem."

"Where are you located these days?"

"I haven't been practicing much. I don't know if you knew, but I lost my license nearly a decade ago. No office. I can come to you, toot toot toot, no problem at all, right away. Just need to get some coffee in me and I will be straight over."

Two hours later, Dr. Foxhide arrived at Nathan's clutching the heavy black leather doctor's bag of a distant era. He stood there in the doorway with a somewhat discomfited, jowly half-smile.

Indicating with a slight move of his head the taxi behind him, Dr. Foxhide said characteristically, "Nathan, toot toot toot. Could you please, toot toot toot, pay the man there?"

Nathan recalled the many expenses associated with Dr. Foxhide, how his father loathed the man and spoke of him as a first-rate chiseler. But Dr. Foxhide had no scruples and sometimes in the business of crime you required someone who didn't give a damn about anything but a buck.

"That's a pretty deep cut there," Dr. Foxhide said upon examining the wound. "That ninja stuff, it's touchy."

Nathan then recollected that both he and his father had been very partial to Dr. Foxhide's deadpan sense of humor.

"I'll stitch ya up, no problem there. It's going to be $500 cash there for today's services, toot toot toot, and I will need you to um, toot toot toot, call me a taxi back to Lawndale and pay that there, toot toot toot."

"That's fine."

"I remember when there was no traffic at all on Olympic Boulevard. You could just sail down the street like you were driving a sled. It doesn't seem that long ago. On the way here, it was a race among snails. Any who, in a week you can give me another call and we'll take out the stitches, or if you know what you're doing, you can take them out yourself. A wound like that, next couple of days, you should take it easy, no horseplay if you know what I mean. You lost some blood. Sleep things off today, stay in, probably better anyways. Now the cash, toot toot toot."

"As if I wasn't going to pay him," thought Nathan sighing.

"Funny thing happened to me yesterday," said Dr. Foxhide. "I was seated on the bus and this older lady comes on, big fat lady dressed real nice. I get up from my seat to offer it to her, all gentleman-like, and she's offended by this. She yells at me hysterically, 'I'm not that old. I'm really not that old. You're older than me. You sit. I'll stand, thank you.' Like I was trying to make some kinda point about her age. Can you believe that? The audacity!"

"She was probably a once famous TV actress," said Nathan.

"Got that right, toot toot toot" mumbled Dr. Foxhide, as he recounted the bills Nathan had just counted out for him.

"That cut you've got there," he went on, "your dad, he came to me with the same sort of slash wound once, but it was on his ass, looked mighty uncomfortable. He couldn't sit down for weeks, not even on the toilet."

"I remember the scar. He was full of scars," recalled Nathan.

"Don't end up full of scars like your dad," said Dr. Foxhide. "It's none of my business, toot toot toot. One or two scars, I dunno, but if you have three significant scars, that's one too many. That tells ya find another line of work."

"Makes sense," said Nathan, now eager to say goodbye to Dr. Foxhide.

As was always the case, Dalton had to work the day after the botched robbery. He had only once in his short career called in sick and it was when he had been truly knocked out by a semi-catastrophic flu. Upon arriving home, he called Nathan and there was no answer. He showered, iced his sore fist, drank two large cups of coffee, and ate four buttered English muffins for breakfast. Then he headed out, sure to be early to work as usual.

In the freshly painted entryway to the building, he encountered Audrey, his excessively sociable neighbor, whom he had gone out with a handful of times, but had since forgotten she existed. She was wearing a green, vintage dress that displayed plenty of leg and thigh.

"Dalton!" she greeted him elatedly, with a friendliness that he assumed she reserved for accomplished performance artists and conceptualists.

"What's cookin', good lookin'?" he said, out of character.

"I've been working on a lot of projects," she said beaming. "You've seen my terrace, haven't you? I've removed all the flowers and replaced them with native Southern California plants. And I've been doing some writing, when I can. But as always, the gallery takes up almost all of my time."

"Anything else?" thought Dalton.

"You're a real night crawler, aren't you?" she asked him.

"Not really," replied Dalton, not knowing what she meant.

"My window is just above the entrance to the parking lot. Sometimes, you come in at crazy hours and then leave again in a couple of hours like you don't sleep at all, for instance, this morning. It was maybe a month ago that you began this pattern of pulling all-nighters once or twice a week. Are you a serial killer or have you found somewhere cool to party to the early morn?"

"I'm a serial killer who likes to party," replied Dalton.

"Really?" Audrey asked probing.

"I've been hanging out with a friend. We've been working on some stuff," he replied vaguely.

"A screenplay," he came up with finally.

"That's great. We should hang out again some time."

Dalton smiled broadly at this invitation. He was proud of the new aura he believed he was projecting: one of newfound poise, street smarts, and a more rugged sensibility to a world that he figured didn't necessarily give a damn about him. He had lived a little. Dalton felt he had taken some big chances and was now being rewarded for them. He had some money in his wallet. A girl that was previously temperate in her interest toward him now wanted to see him once more, though he wasn't sure if he wanted to go out with her again.

This was a brand new Dalton Everest, he was certain of, not the same old one who cowered at times before females. A girl he had once gone out on a date with had called him "repressed," when he had objected to her calling some of her friends and acquaintances, "bitches and whores." Maybe "repressed" had been an accurate description of him at the time, but it wasn't anymore. Audrey had once called him "sensitive," when she had months ago stated that he carried himself like a high school teacher and apparently he had then grimaced with shame. In addition, he had been called "short" and "tiny" repeatedly by girls who were not much taller than him. Melanee had done this more than once and look what had happened to her.

But this thought threw a suddenly disturbed expression on Dalton's face, mid-conversation.

"We don't need to hang out, if you are busy at all hours working on your screenplay," said Audrey, her expression now somewhat soured at Dalton's nonresponse to her mentioning that they should get together again.

"I would love to hang out with you," said Dalton return-ing to Earth. "We should go out for a drink or something soon. Recently, I have discovered some incredible bars that are more fun than a new puppy. But, right now, yeah, I'm encumbered by this screenplay project. I haven't been getting much sleep and I'm nuts. Say, I will give you a call in a month or whatever when I'm closer to putting this thing to bed."

"Sure," replied Audrey, fake smile and all, walking past him insulted.

Dalton realized that he had handled that poorly, and for the rest of the day it bothered the hell out of him, just as it would have before his recently changed disposition.

Upon returning home that evening, Dalton called Nathan to see what had become of him.

"You're still alive? You're not a decomposing corpse on the mean streets of Santa Monica?" asked Dalton.

"I'm watching *The Killing*. It's an early Stanley Kubrick flick, a black and white film noir about a horse track heist. Marie Windsor is such a royal bad-ass in this film. Have you heard of Sterling Hayden? He's the lead."

"I am familiar with Stanley Kubrick. Do you still have that arm with the hole in it?

"Wasn't a problem, had that patched up. Did you know that we've made the local TV news? Most of the story was the unimpressive credits of the TV producer, Milton Newski, who owned the house. Otherwise, they claimed it was an aggravated assault and attempted rape, no discussion of an attempted bur-glary. They mentioned that the girl used an Emmy Award as a weapon to fight off her would-be attacker."

"Attempted rape! What's that about?"

"The girl must have pulled that out of a hat," said Nathan.

"I've been meaning to ask you, but didn't get a chance while we were running from the po po: how did you end up getting locked in that garage?"

"I'm still processing a couple of blunders I made. Thanks again for getting me out of a tight spot. As for saving each other's necks, we're even now."

"Could there be some heat from this attempted rape, assault thing showing up on the news? You're always very devil-may-care about this sort of stuff."

"First, I like that you call it heat," said Nathan jokingly. "That's very vintage crime. You're starting to nail the lingo and I'm impressed. Did you toss that sweater that you were wearing?"

"Yes. I got rid of it just after we split up."

"As I was saying, you are a pro. I don't think anyone got a good enough look at us, just the stolen minivan. Even if they had a description of us, what are they going to do with it? They would have had to grab us on the spot."

"Before I got into this line of work, I had this preposterous assumption that the police investigated crimes and tried to solve them. I don't know what I was thinking or where I got that ludicrous idea."

"That's pure folly. Cops don't care about us and our petty criminality. Speaking of, something else has already come up. It's close to my place in Silver Lake. We have a little time on this one. The woman and her daughter are out of town for a week. I'm going to rest this arm over the weekend. How about, be ready Monday night to scope the place out? Then, if all is hunky dory, we'll hit the place next Tuesday night. This time, though, you are going in."

"Now, why would you want me to do that?"

"I want to provide a well-rounded education. You've got to be all in with this thing. Driving is just a small part of the whole enterprise. There's more money in it for you, if you do the actual robbing. I will give you all the pointers you need as far as how to go about it and what to grab and also provide you with an unlocked door."

"I'll have to think about it."

"Okay, see you Monday then."

That weekend Dalton went to Melrose Avenue and the Beverly Center to buy clothes for himself, the first time he had done so in three years.

By Monday evening, he had already psyched himself into the idea of being the actual burglar for the next job and that night he drove Nathan in his own car up the steep, curvy streets of the Silver Lake hills, overlooking the Silver Lake Reservoir, to a small street called Lanterman Terrace, where they cased a house painted an unusual shade of orange. Nathan described this job as "a piece of cake." There was no alarm, no dog, no fence, and likely no private security in the area. He did not skimp in his detailed instructions on what was generally worth stealing and what was best left behind.

The next evening, they pulled in front of the house again in a stolen Toyota 4Runner SUV and both got out. In the past, Nathan had said that the appropriate attire for crime was dark colors with nothing that stuck out as looking particularly criminal, like a knit hat or a dark ski jacket. On this cold evening, Dalton wore his brand new light grey pin-striped long sleeve shirt under his favorite worn, brown corduroy jacket, along with an old pair of Levi's. It was an outfit that definitely didn't advertise criminality.

"I'm going to be a little daring and hit the front door here," said Nathan as they approached the house. "Then, I will go in with you and then come back out to the car and wait."

Nathan pulled out a tiny tool and casually went to work on the lock. It was open in twenty seconds, but once open, there was an additional chain lock behind it.

"I should have gone through the back door," said Nathan whipping out a screwdriver.

It took another minute to unscrew the chain lock and they were in. Nathan closed the door behind them and they switched on their flashlights. The living room walls were painted burgundy and the Silver Lake bohemian vibe of the place, which was crammed with doodads, was somewhat intimidating in the near dark with its bloody Catholic themed artwork and velveteen covered sofa, which had a couple of fluffy white Persian cats perched on it staring at them with yellow eyes.

"Knock yourself out with this one," said Nathan exiting the house.

Following his instructions, Dalton stumbled around the enormous cluttered living room in an effort to locate the bedroom, where Nathan had said the majority of steal-worthy possessions were usually found. But first, he came upon the kitchen and breakfast nook, which were eccentrically decorated with Japanese toys. He turned on his tail and found the bedroom, which was dominated by a huge bed covered in crushed velvet blankets and pillows and surrounded by dark blue painted furniture weighed down with half melted botanica candles and other Catholic paraphernalia.

"This lady is not religious," thought Dalton. "She just overindulged in the ready availability in this neighborhood of this particular crap aesthetic."

Spacing out for a second, Dalton returned to the thievery aspect of what he was doing, as he noticed an acoustic guitar in one corner, though it was covered with band stickers. On the way out, he would decide whether to grab that or not. He then began rummaging through all the drawers as Nathan had stressed and discovered the woman's jewelry. But the colorful Bakelite necklaces, skull earrings, and hair pins in the shapes of scarabs seemed to Dalton to have little value. Still, he emptied a whole drawer of the stuff into a garbage bag. He noticed a collection of graphic novels and paperback books on a rickety wooden bookshelf, but as he scanned the titles, he realized that wasn't what he was supposed to be looking for. After dumping a couple of other items of questionable worth into his bag, he decided that he was done with the bedroom and moved on through the narrow hallway past a pretty, white-tiled bathroom, also cluttered with botanica candles, leading to a second bedroom.

The black walls of the second bedroom at first startled Dalton, but then after a once over, he realized from the stuffed animals and notebooks that this was the room of a kid and became temporarily sick to his stomach.

"How the hell do I find myself in a kid's room looking for stuff to steal?" he asked himself.

He then had a major freak-out consisting partially of bottled up angst and petrifying fear at the clearly treacherous position he had put himself into for the most questionable of purposes. Feeling something behind him, Dalton almost stepped on one of the cats that was rubbing itself against the back of his legs.

Stamping out of the house, he put on the brakes, went back into the main bedroom, grabbed the guitar and left. Outside, it was quiet, cold, and hazy. Entering the stolen SUV with a tiny bag of loot and the guitar, Dalton was still floundering emotionally.

"This one was a washout," sputtered Dalton. "I got to the kid's room and froze up. Maybe, I'm not cut out for this."

Nathan did not bother to conceal his annoyance.

Looking through the contents of the bag with his flashlight, he irritably glanced at each piece of jewelry and declared it all to be junk.

Then he looked at Dalton square in the eyes and said somewhat accusingly in hushed tones, "You were in that house forever. You're telling me, there is nothing of value in there?"

"This woman is a musician or artist I guess. I don't know. She reads Neil Gaiman books and I would say everything in the house was bought in a short radius of here between Los Feliz and those little crappy stores on Sunset Boulevard in Echo Park. I don't think this woman is rich, and I don't know that we should be in her house stealing from her."

"Look at the house," argued Nathan. "This woman is a rich divorcee. She's not loaded down with trunks full of money like that producer in the last house we hit, but you can't make the case that she's not wealthy. It's still dark and I haven't heard a peep in all this time, so we're going to go back in and go to town."

"What about the guitar?" asked Dalton. "Should I just bring that back?"

"Yes. Grab that piece of rubbish and put it back."

They quickly went back in the house and Nathan scampered through the living room to the main bedroom and began to thoroughly delve through the drawers.

"It's true that this woman has been unsparing in keeping every piece of junk that she ever came upon in her life," said Nathan.

Looking under the bed, he pulled out a tiny ring box and opened it.

"A Bulgari diamond, not too bad," said Nathan changing his tune.

"But that's her wedding ring," argued Dalton.

"She's no longer married," said Nathan. "There is no guy stuff in this house. She lives here with her 15-year-old daughter. I did some research. If you all of a sudden want to sprout a conscience, doing it in the middle of a job, the first one where you went in on your own is maybe not the best time."

Nathan jumped as a cat rubbed itself against the back of his legs.

"This is all we need," said Nathan referring to the wedding ring. "Let's scram."

On their way back to drop off the stolen Toyota, the two of them kept silent. Dalton was obviously disconcerted about the experience.

"It's not usually like that," said Nathan. "Almost anyone with a big house has plenty of valuables lying around. I can see how it threw you for a loop with those yellow-eyed cats. In the dark, sometimes these places can look like haunted houses. I apologize for getting perturbed."

Compared to Nathan's former accomplices, Dalton had been exemplary and in another league, though of course not on this job. Nathan was used to being petulant and bossy to those who worked for him, but he knew that wasn't going to fly with Dalton, where the goal was not simply to use and then dispose of him, but to have a real pal to lean on over the long run. This blending of business and friendship was a sticky minefield, he considered.

"Really, I was the one who made a scene," admitted Dalton. "I was the one acting like Shelley Winters, no fault of yours."

"Thursday night, 9 pm, I have a meeting with a jewelry buyer at his apartment in West Hollywood. Why don't you come along and keep me company? If everything is square with this fella, it could be a pretty penny for the both of us."

"Why not," said Dalton.

A couple of nights later, Dalton and Nathan found the apartment of the jewelry buyer, Borislav, on Ogden Drive, off of Santa Monica Boulevard, and speculated that the Mazda parked in front of it with the GETN8KD vanity plate was his. After finding a parking space three blocks away, they hiked back and were buzzed into the apartment, taking an elevator to the sixth floor.

Borislav, who Nathan had mentioned he knew little about, opened the door and gave them a thorough sizing up with a pouty-lipped expression on his face, shaking hands with them in a robotic fashion. A tall, well-built fellow with a dumb-looking partly shaved haircut, Borislav looked to be in his mid-twenties, or younger, and there was nothing about him that suggested "jewelry smuggler." His apartment had a huge rectangular living room, where stood another equally long-limbed fellow, who might have been Borislav's brother, and a somewhat older, intense looking blonde girl with her hair wrapped in a tight bun. The maybe-brother barely acknowledged them, while the blonde took an immediate interest in both Nathan and Dalton.

"My name is Anya," she said with a Russian accent out of a spy film.

"You," she said pointing to Nathan, "are interesting, complex, filled with secrets, almost impenetrable. It's a compelling face you possess."

"Much obliged," said Nathan.

"And you," she said turning to Dalton dramatically, "I have a great amount of sympathy for you. I am so sorry about ... everything."

"What is that supposed to mean?" asked Dalton aghast.

"My sister, she's a seer," said Borislav, with an accent that was like thick borscht, as he stood at a desk concentrating on his computer screen and not raising his eyes from it. "She will tell you your future, your past, and all kinds of things you probably don't want to know."

"You two are entwined," continued Anya, as if she was on a stage in front of a nineteenth-century audience of gape-mouthed villagers. "You have not known each other long, but both of your futures are inexorably tied to each other."

"I guess that might all be true," said Dalton skeptically, "but it seems broad enough that you could say it to almost anyone."

"You are a school teacher and grew up in Los Angeles," Anya added. "You do not have a lover and have never really had one. At the moment, you are unfocused. Uncomfortable situations like this one, you often mark them with your humor. You are a very funny man."

"I'm sold," said Nathan attempting to break the eerie mood. "She's reading you like a billboard."

"But there is a great sadness behind your eyes," added Anya, still speaking to Dalton. "It's heartbreaking when someone takes the wrong path, one that was clearly not chosen for them. It doesn't have to be that way."

Neither Nathan nor Dalton were too keen on having anyone peer into their souls, and both had grown steadily more unnerved by the strangeness of this meeting and its lack of any relation to why they had come there.

"Borislav, you're a rock collector, no?" asked Nathan, attempting to cut off the tea leaf reading.

"Show me what you've got," replied Borislav, finally showing a modicum of interest.

Pulling out a small black case from his inner jacket pocket, Nathan opened it and pulled out another fancy case from within, placed it on Borislav's desk and opened that. Arrayed in the velvet case were 19 diamonds. Six were diamond rings, and one was three times the size of the others.

"It's hot stuff, isn't it?" said Borislav, glancing at the diamonds. "You probably can't sell this to almost anyone. The insurance guys would catch up with you quick. I have a guy in Syria, who is a big diamond buyer. He might be interested in these rocks. But I am sure you can appreciate that it's not easy to get these to Syria. I can offer you eight thousand cash for all of them."

"I was told you were a serious buyer," answered Nathan. "Those diamonds are worth a couple hundred thousand. The least I would sell them for would be fifty grand, cash of course. If you can come up with that sort of dough, let me know."

He gathered them up and placed them back in the case in his jacket pocket.

"And what's the little guy staring at?" asked Borislav, referring to Dalton. "Why do you bring this little guy around with you if you think you are a big cheese?"

"No reason to insult anyone ..." replied Nathan, but as he said it, an incensed Dalton lunged at Borislav throwing a wild punch at his face, though missing by a wide margin. The two of them then grabbed each other by the arms. A look of astonishment on his face, Borislav used his superior strength to slam Dalton against his desk, but Dalton held onto him and delivered several hard punches to his kidneys causing Borislav to squeal. The guy who was likely Borislav's brother then jumped into the skirmish, forcing Nathan to do the same out of fairness. It was then a mess of grabbing and pushing between the four of them, Anya getting out of the way and looking on from a distance. Both Nathan and the fellow they assumed was Borislav's brother were trying to untangle them, but in the process this maybe-brother threw a punch at Dalton, hitting him on the forearm. Then dislodging himself from Borislav's grip, Dalton threw an uppercut that connected with the maybe-brother's chin.

"Lay off!" yelled Nathan, yanking Dalton away from them, pulling him behind him in a protective manner and then pushing Borislav and the maybe-brother back.

"Could you calm your surly ass down?" he ordered Dalton.

But cooler heads did not prevail as the maybe-brother with the sore chin attempted to get around Nathan and lunge at Dalton. Nathan caught his arm and Dalton punched him in the ribs.

"Holy fuck!" exclaimed the maybe-brother clutching his ribcage as he crumbled to the ground.

"Let's beat it!" exclaimed Nathan, using Dalton's decisive punch to the ribs as an excuse to get the hell out of there.

Still pausing for a second to deliberate with the manly part of himself whether he should additionally attempt to finish off Borislav, Dalton finally realized he had taken this as far as it needed to go and left in rapid fashion with Nathan, Borislav yelling something insulting in Russian as they slammed the door behind them.

Hurrying down an endless dark and grimy staircase, Nathan exclaimed to Dalton, who was feeling very macho and so was not as inclined to rush, "Those pinkos most assuredly have guns somewhere in that apartment, so you need to get it in gear."

Once it was determined that they were not being followed as they drove back to Los Feliz in Nathan's Audi, Dalton began to gloat, "Is there any way to calculate the sheer amount of ass I just kicked?"

"I don't see what the point of all that was."

"Nathan, I really didn't feel like the deal was going down as expected," said Dalton in a tone of voice that was not his own. "You were pretty far off on price. Buttislav thinks he can start talking smack to me and I shut him up, no harm, no foul."

"Those punk-ass kids clearly were diamond smugglers and they might very well have gotten back to me with a better offer and because I have no clue what to do with these rocks, I might have taken it. He was low balling me, but that's how these things go. Those kids were legit and you played them all wrong by taking things personally and making like Bruce Lee. The way you handled it, our wallets are lighter, you're bruised up and full of pride, and we are still holding onto a heap of diamonds with no buyer."

"Well, if you have to put it that way," said Dalton, alighting back to Earth with his wings singed.

~ 11 ~

POST-PRODUCTION

Shambling into the division at 7 am, already with a ruffled look about him, Detective Talbert was not at all surprised to find two new cases on his desk.

"Holy frijoles!" he said aloud. "It's going to be petty-ass bullshit."

Skimming the first one, he sighed, it was a gang case. Two men had barged into a house guns drawn in Highland Park and the neighbors had reported it, but no report at all from the house in question whose occupants had been completely unresponsive to queries from the uniformed cops who'd interviewed them. Obviously, thought Talbert, this was a gang or drug-related dispute with no shots fired, and it had fallen onto his desk because the gang unit had deemed it unworthy of their time. He had gotten wind that some of the lamer cases that had landed on his desk had been somehow passed on by the gang unit, though it was possibly a spurious rumor.

"Hot shot assholes!" he muttered to himself.

The gang unit cops were almost all younger than Talbert, who was 38, and some of them had been on the force for just a few years. He didn't envy them, he just thought they were vastly overrated and cocksure, "a bunch of fuckheads in sunglasses and baseball caps," he had once called them.

The other case struck him as atypical, a tangle of ostensibly unrelated criminality barely glued together. A post-it note on the file from Captain Shaw said "Talbert, take a gander at this one!"

"What the hell does that mean?" he said under his breath.

Six cars of varying makes and models had been reported stolen in East Hollywood and Los Feliz and then had been returned undamaged to basically the same spot where they had been taken or nearby over the last three months.

Then, an additional attached case involved an aggravated assault and attempted rape in the Pacific Palisades at the home of a Hollywood producer, Milton Newski. His daughter, Tamara, had claimed that two white males had cut the power and telephone lines to her father's house, broke in and one of them had attempted to rape her, but she had struck him with an Emmy Award and both white males had then fled. Her boyfriend, Mark Teitelbaum, had arrived during the fracas and had been attacked by one of the assailants causing a minor concussion.

"What kind of crazy bull pucky is that?" Talbert muttered to himself.

The description of the two white males in the report was next to nothing: one had been wearing a striped sweater, the accused rapist had curly hair, the color of his hair was not mentioned. Also, there were no details about the attempted rape. The report noted that the daughter had been sketchy in her description of the events, changing her story twice over three interviews. The boyfriend had been struck from behind and had not seen either perpetrator. A neighbor had reported seeing the culprits pull away in a minivan. He had also mentioned the striped sweater and had said one was short, one was tall; that was it.

There had been nearly no follow-up on the case, except for the discovery four days later of a stolen minivan, which had been towed by the city of Santa Monica, and reported stolen by the owner who lived in East Hollywood in the area of the before-mentioned car thievery. The neighbor who had been a witness to the two perps fleeing from the Hollywood producer's home had said they had done so in a green minivan, no make or model.

A detective from the Santa Monica Police had determined that the recovered stolen green minivan was likely used and ditched by the culprits behind the aggravated assault and attempted rape, which had taken place a mere ten-minute drive away from where the minivan had been left.

The only link between the aggravated assault and attempted rape case and the car thievery cases on the other side of town was the neighborhood from which the minivan was taken.

"What a lot of hooey!" pondered Talbert. "This is some half-ass investigative work. Maybe some lowlifes might have stolen a minivan and ended up on the other side of town trying to maybe rape some girl, but probably not, because she doesn't seem to want to say nothin' about it because she maybe knew these dickweeds and one of them decked her boyfriend."

Realizing that that summation was nonsense, Talbert reread the whole file.

"The unusual pattern of car thievery is likely tied to robberies of some sort," deliberated Talbert. "But the minivan stolen from the same neighborhood, then driven to the scene of this baffling crime by these young white guys, one of them wearing a striped sweater, then dumped not so far away after the police were en route–I don't know what the fuck that's about."

The case was at the very least intriguing, and somebody was up to something crooked and indefinable.

"Stealing a minivan to commit rape or beat up some-one's boyfriend across town; that don't make no sense," he thought continuing to hammer away at it. "A minivan is useful for transporting something large, but not the girl. Maybe, they were up to something else."

The case was stuck in his brain and filling up the whole of it.

"I'm going to ignore this wishy-washy gang case for now," thought Talbert. "But this other one, I'm going to hit it full stride."

A couple of hours later, Talbert was pressing the entry button at the gate of the Pacific Palisades mansion of Hollywood producer Milton Newski, determined to fish some piece of use-ful evidence from Newski's daughter, Tamara, who was clearly holding something back. His hunch was that something poten-tially embarrassing was causing her to give the police as little information as possible.

"Hi ya," said Tamara opening the door for Talbert.

A short girl with long brown hair and an olive complex-ion, Tamara struck Talbert as a two-timing, stone cold liar and harpy, of that much he was quite sure.

"As I mentioned on the phone," said Talbert, "we believe those men who came in here and attacked you and your boyfriend were involved in a series of car robberies. With this new evidence in hand, I need you to give me a detailed account of what all happened that night?"

Standing in a living room decked out pompously with fake marble and a bust of Julius Caesar in a style of Roman ex-cess, Tamara made no effort to offer Talbert a seat, scowled at his inquiry, and sped through her account of the events.

"In the early morning, I was awoken by a noise and couldn't get the lights to come on," she said indifferently. "I found a flashlight, entered the living room and there were two men standing there."

"Tell me exactly your recollection of their appearance with as much detail as possible."

"It was pitch dark. One had curly hair. The other guy was short and was wearing a navy blue sweater with a white stripe."

"In the initial interview you stated that the perpetrator with the curly hair attempted to rape you. We can't do anything with the description you gave us. It could be any two white men on the planet that came in here. The curly haired one, was he muscular, skinny, fat, light-skinned? Did you catch the color of his eyes? Did he have freckles, moles, a tattoo, bad teeth, a receding hairline, anything?"

"Look, it was dark. I couldn't see them."

"But you had a flashlight."

"They knocked it out of my hands."

"I don't recall that you mentioned that in any of the previous interviews."

"I don't know. Maybe no one asked."

"Is there a reason that you don't want the police to pursue these two men?"

"Pardon my French, but I don't really give a flying fuck if you ever find these two creeps and I don't expect it will ever happen. The police are a bunch of nitwits. You are the third cop to come here and harass me. If you'll excuse me, I have a ton of calls and emails to get back to."

"Let me just remind you that falsifying a police report is a crime."

"Wearing a suit as ugly as that is a crime."

As he let himself out, Talbert pictured himself bashing the girl's face in with the blunt end of his pistol.

"Ain't nothin' that girl said that wasn't a lie," raged Talbert to himself. "Every single word out of her princessy mouth was concentrated bullshit. Don't mean a damn thing, though. This case is about two white perps stealing cars to commit robberies. They cut the power and phone lines to kill the alarm, so they ain't small timers. I could stake out the neighborhood where they are stealing the cars from, but the distance seems too wide and the car swiping is too irregular. But now that I'm on their ass, better watch out."

On the eternal drive back to the Eastside, heading north on the 405 freeway through the patchy green, light brown, and little spots of yellow of the Santa Monica Mountains, and then along the 101 racing through the Valley, Talbert determined that one or more of the car thieves probably lived or worked in the East Hollywood area or nearby. He decided he would utilize an old fashioned approach and canvass the area, ask neighbors in the vicinity of the car thefts if they had noticed any suspicious activity. In Talbert's past investigations, it had been an occasional case breaker, and additionally, it was good exercise walking around for hours.

Late afternoon, he parked on gloomy, despondent Normandie Avenue, where the minivan had been swiped. He figured someone might have seen something from one of the balconies of the many giant apartment buildings on the street. In the first three buildings, knocking on nearly a hundred doors and speaking to about thirty folks, Talbert came up with squat. One elderly Armenian man who spoke halting English claimed to have seen what might have been a car theft from his balcony, but he could provide no details other than "maybe the car was brown." That wasn't much to go on. Otherwise, he spoke to several spooked illegal immigrants, one cockeyed old man, a couple of residents with apartments that wreaked of marijuana and one perhaps flirtatious or friendly Thai girl, who repeated twice, "you're so tall." Talbert also met numerous Armenian housewives, some of whom were not terribly friendly.

The next day, he hoped to canvass the streets surrounding at least three of the car thefts. Starting in the morning, he found most people to be at work, but kept at it, noting on a pad of paper the house and apartments, where no one had been. After a few hours of work and a lengthy lunch break spent at Machos Tacos on Vermont Avenue, Talbert knocked on the door of a duplex on Talmadge Avenue and Nathan answered the door.

"Detective Talbert, LAPD," he said introducing himself.

A hollow feeling in the pit of Nathan's stomach and a rapidly accelerated heartbeat made it difficult to present an innocent smile.

"We're investigating several car thefts in the neighborhood, one was just a couple of blocks away. Have you noticed anything out of the ordinary during late night hours?"

"Nope, I haven't seen anything. Usually, I'm asleep."

"You get up early? What do you do?" Talbert inquired.

"I'm in post-production."

There was something a tad off about the young man, Talbert considered. The smile seemed overly forced and he thought he noticed a nervous twitch when the man spoke. He waited for a few seconds saying nothing and noticed Nathan's smile coming and going, as if he was trying very hard to keep it on his face. Might as well continue the conversation, he decided, as this young man seemed to have something to spill.

"A couple of guys have been hotwiring cars in the area. Do you own a car that you park on the street?"

"Yes sir, I do."

Again, the calling him "sir" seemed very forced, but some people acted nervously in the presence of police.

"I would suggest keeping an eye on your car and remember to lock it. Could I get your name?"

"Nathan Lyme," he revealed hesitantly.

Talbert wrote it down on his pad, where he had written some useless notes: one man had seen a group of teenagers running around the neighborhood in the evening, a lady mentioned a homeless man that she believed was breaking into cars. But Nathan Lyme's was the only name he had written on his note pad, and he wasn't sure why he'd asked for it.

"If I see anything, I will be sure to call the police," said Nathan, attempting to keep it together.

"Thank you, please do that," said Talbert departing.

After shutting the door, Nathan felt dizzy, sat down and held his head in his hands. What an idiotic mistake it had been to steal all the cars in a twenty block radius of his home, he now saw clearly. And the one car that he had boosted a couple of blocks away had been an abysmal blunder. Also, with no other apparent choice, he had just given his name to a cop investigating crimes he had committed.

"He walked right up to my door," thought Nathan trying to regain his cool, but at the same time keep a lucid perception of what had just occurred. "And I revealed myself by nearly breaking down in front of him. That cop must have something on me. It can't be a coincidence. But then he didn't reveal his hand either. Son of a ... "

After many hours of sitting around drinking Scotch, eating frozen cheese enchiladas from Trader Joe's and brooding over his next move, Nathan resolved to lay low for a spell, abandon the burglary plans for the evening with a health excuse and try and manage to keep everything from Dalton, so as not to scare him off.

Nathan looked at his telephone with dread.

"It's probably not bugged," he pondered. "Of course, going out and using a public phone could be even more suspicious, if they were tailing me."

"But I don't want to turn into a paranoid," he said aloud to himself. He rang Dalton.

"I need to call it off for tonight," said Nathan. "I've got a stomach bug."

"Oh, okay," replied Dalton surprised, "fine with me."

"I will give you a call when I get over this and we'll reschedule."

Nathan was unusually curt and Dalton didn't know what to make of it, but was pleased, and at the same time, somewhat let down that the burglary had been called off. It just meant that his life would be back to normal for a few days and there was both the good and the slightly boring in that.

Meanwhile, for three more days, Talbert combed the neighborhood, not once recalling his brief conversation with Nathan, in an instant forgotten. Sunny and virtually cloudless, these November days were exceedingly pleasant and though the work was slow and painstaking, Talbert believed it was in this way, searching long and far, that cases were solved, when there wasn't a lot of evidence to go on. And so it was that on a Thursday afternoon he knocked on the door of an apartment on Franklin Avenue and spoke with a prematurely gray haired, forty-something-year-old man whose car had been stolen in front of his apartment.

"I didn't bother to report it to the police," explained the man. "I hadn't noticed the car had been stolen, but I saw these two thieves, strange in that they didn't look at all like criminals, return the car just a few spaces down from where I had parked it. They couldn't see me at all because I was looking through that tiny upstairs window, but I saw them as clear as if they were standing on my shoes."

Talbert's eyes nearly popped out of his head.

"Could you tell me every detail that you can recall about the appearance of the two thieves and do you mind if I tape it?"

He pulled out a tape recorder and pushed record.

"Absolutely. The one was lugging a garbage bag, which he pulled out of my backseat, crazy that, and he was a tall bugger, maybe six feet, even a little taller, kind of built, curly light brown hair. They were both white young men in their twenties I would conjecture."

Smiling wide, Talbert was confident that the witness was describing the same two perps who had stolen the minivan and had inexplicably ended up at the TV producer's home in the Palisades.

"I guess you could say the taller one sported the sharp appearance of a TV actor, pretty wide shoulders, a pronounced chin. I was thinking to call the police, so I was careful to note everything I could about them. But my car was in the same shape that it had been before they took it. They even locked the doors."

"What about the other guy?" asked Talbert.

"Short, much shorter. He was the driver. He had brown hair parted, darker hair than the other guy, kind of skinny. It looked like he was doing a lot of talking, but I couldn't hear him from the window. He was wearing a brown corduroy jacket. It could have been an old one and he had on dark pants that didn't match at all with the jacket. The main thing that stuck out about him was that he was not much more than five feet tall, a little stump of a guy."

"I know it was a distance. But did you notice any tattoos, bad teeth, a limp?"

"No, I think that's about all I have on those two."

"Can I get your name?"

"Ronald Mint."

"Mr. Mint, these two may have looked fairly harmless, but they are suspected of stealing numerous cars in the area and being involved in an attempted rape and aggravated assault. It would be great if I could drive you over to the police station and have you take a look at some photos. It won't take more than a couple of hours of your time."

"I can do that," replied Mr. Mint, the sort of accommodating witness that was like a rainbow with a pot of gold to the police.

At the division, Mr. Mint went through a pile of mug books, but nobody stood out. While awaiting the arrival of a sketch artist, Talbert took him out for coffee and Mr. Mint showed an enthusiastic interest in everything LAPD related and seemed to be enjoying the whole day's experience. Into the early evening, he and the sketch artist worked on approximating the images of the two car thieves and in the end, all were pleased with the results. Talbert felt he had finally turned a corner on the case.

Though, for the next couple of days he found himself in possession of the same profiles with diddly-squat to add to them, despite phone interviews with both Tamara's now ex-boyfriend, the one who had been decked by one of the assailants and who repeated his assertion that he had not seen them at all, and the neighbor, who had been a witness to their fleeing the house. The neighbor's description, despite some uncertainty on a few details, was nearly the same as Mr. Mint's.

Then, it came, a call to the station from Hollywood Division. A girl had shown up there familiar, she said, with both of the sketched criminals on the posted flyer, worried about a missing friend, who she claimed was linked to both men. Not sure what to make of it, Talbert carefully considered the few bits of seemingly unrelated facts he had gleaned from the officer he spoke with, as he called up and made an appointment with Allison Turnbull and then drove to her apartment in Hollywood.

At the door of a dirt-flecked pink apartment building on Fountain Avenue, a pretty blonde girl answered. Based on a few prior experiences, Talbert had concluded that every above average looking blonde girl in the city of Los Angeles was an obnoxious brat.

"Ma'am, Detective Talbert, LAPD."

"Come in," said Allison distraught.

"I understand you recognized the two criminals in the sketch at the police station."

"Yes, I know them. A friend of my former roommate, this little gutter punk kid named Sam showed up here yesterday. He was arrested for somethingerother and at the police station he saw the drawings and recognized Nathan, who he had seen with my former roommate, Melanee, who disappeared a couple of months ago. Sam had been wondering what happened to her."

Allison began to tear up.

"I went to the police station and saw the drawings too," she continued. "That's Nathan Lyme, who Melanee had had some kind of a relationship with."

The name, Nathan Lyme, struck Talbert as familiar, but he couldn't place it.

"Not only did the one drawing look like Nathan, but the other guy is named Dalton, a friend of Nathan's, who also went out with my former roommate a handful of times. She was kind of slutty."

"You have a last name for the other guy?" asked Talbert.

"No, but I met him and talked to him a few times when he was waiting here for her to get ready. He's a high school teacher, kind of fidgety. He didn't seem capable of any of the crimes mentioned on the flyer. But it's him. I think they are both friends, though I never saw them together."

Talbert didn't yet see any definitive connection between his case and Allison's missing roommate with the two boyfriends.

"So, you believe something befell this roommate and you believe these two are responsible?"

"I thought my roommate suddenly went back to France, but she's dead," said Allison, eyes fixated on an image in her head. "They showed me photos of the corpse. I couldn't really tell from the body. They said there was barely a head attached. But the clothes! They were hers. They had her boots. Those cut-off shirts. They said she fell off a cliff and had never been identified."

Allison burst into tears.

The maybe-dead roommate meant next to nothing to Talbert and crying, emotional blonde girls always exasperated him.

"Running around like a ho, boyfriends up to her ears, what good could possibly come of the dumb-as-nails roommate," he thought to himself.

He had to proceed, though. This witness evidently thought she knew the two. This was probably somebody in Hollywood Division's case, if it was anybody's case.

"Um. I'm going to ask you some questions based on what I've got on the two men in the sketch. Let me know if anything rings a bell. Do these guys steal cars?"

"Nathan always seemed like he could be an international spy or something. He might steal cars. I don't know. I can't picture Dalton stealing a car."

"This girl has got an eggplant upstairs," thought Talbert. "Nobody's an international spy and if they were, they wouldn't be hanging out with your tramp roommate, no way."

"Do you know where either of them lives?" he asked.

"I think Nathan lives nearby. I have his number."

Allison went to retrieve the telephone number, but couldn't find it, while Talbert stared at the white wall struck bored and wishing to escape. Though, he couldn't just skip out of there.

"Tell me, why do you suspect that these two had something to do with the disappearance or death of your former roommate?"

"It can't just be a coincidence that Melanee is dead and that there is a wanted poster of Nathan and Dalton up at the police station," replied Allison defensively. "Nathan came over the day before she disappeared months ago and she may have gone out with Dalton or him that evening. When I called Nathan asking if he knew where she was, he seemed positive that she had just left the country, leaving all of her crap at my place, without saying goodbye to anyone."

She became teary-eyed again.

It was such a mishmash, contemplated Talbert.

"Could you tell me exactly what both of them look like with as much detail as possible?"

Allison's take was unexpectedly dead-on with Mr. Mint's description including the addition that Dalton, the short one, had dirty fingernails and wore loafers or boots with small heels. Nathan, she related, was stylishly attired: dress shirts, slacks, suits occasionally. Talbert's head spun around at the realization that he was indeed on to something, and that Allison's bewildering story was apparently tied to the perps he was after. He became more cordial and began taping everything. Allison couldn't remember her former roommate's or Dalton's last names, another example of brainlessness to Talbert. But he had the name, Nathan Lyme, which he could run through the system. Probably nothing would come up, he suspected. However, the full name made him feel like he had finally broke out of a thick forest entering a wide meadow and his prey was just a short distance off begging to be collared.

"These two white dudes, whatever they're up to, best get set to make some license plates," he told himself upon leaving Allison's pad.

The crimes, however, were disparate, really a mess of illegal activity with no evident pattern. The sort of scum who murder girls, by pushing them off a cliff no less, whoever those guys are, don't as a rule steal cars and break into houses, reasoned Talbert. Though, in this case, there was the allegation of an attempted rape with zero evidence to back it up and an unreliable victim, which added another layer of confounding to the conflicting verifiable facts that he had to work with.

"Crazy white idiots high on crack might do some of that stuff," surmised Talbert as he drove across the Fletcher Drive

Bridge, which spanned a trickling L.A. River, "but they would never return stolen cars or know how to or even think to disable an alarm. Throwing this trampy girl off a cliff, don't see where that fits in. One could have been jealous of the other. But then the producer's house incident happened afterwards and involved the both of them. That don't make a lick of sense. Only thing to do is locate this Nathan Lyme and then sit on him."

Back at Northwest Division, he proceeded directly to the coffee machine and bumped into Officer Peete, one of very few African-American cops at the station, who Talbert didn't much care for and didn't trust at all, for no definable reason.

"Talbert, what's goin' on?"

"Not much, working an unusual case, a couple of white boys going around committing a lot of random crimes, everywhichwhere in the city."

"I'm so glad to be out of Southeast Division," related Officer Peete. "I can run with the fools around here. Feared for my life at times working Southeast. All the drug dealers were packing semi-automatics. Those Black gangs are straight up more frightening than the homiez in these parts."

"Is that so?" replied Talbert, wondering what Peete's reminiscences had to do with what he had just said.

"Yeah. I like it here. Don't get me wrong. A beat in the suburbs, I wouldn't care for that. But I also want to stay the hell out the hood."

"Scared of niggas?" asked Talbert.

"Lot of good guys around here," went on Peete, as if he hadn't heard the question, "Rick, Jack, Javier, all pals, spend a lot of time just joking around."

"I'll see you later," said Talbert brusquely as he headed to his desk.

Sitting down, he nonchalantly picked up his note pad and flipped through it. Written prominently by itself on one of the pages was the name, Nathan Lyme.

"Did I meet this son of a bitch? How the beeswax did that name get there?" he thought hard.

Possibly, it was someone he'd interviewed in the neighborhood of the car robberies, or it could have been a name from a previous case, since his notes were always a mess.

"Holy hamburger buns and a shit shake," he said to himself.

~ 12 ~

THE UNVEILING OF HIS SECRET

Drifting into class four minutes late, casually placing his Calvin Klein designer shades in a fancy case on his desk and hanging his $420 leather jacket, Dalton, unshaved, was in the process of unveiling a new persona that caused his students to snicker. The shaving every three days look he had begun a couple of weeks previous. After a recent successful burglary of a Hollywood Hills home in which Dalton had done the actual burglarizing and had come away with $3200 in cash, along with a wealth of jewelry and several designer handbags, he had purchased the sunglasses and the leather jacket at a pricey store on La Brea Avenue. Briefly, he had debated if he might wear them to school, deciding, "Why the hell not?" In front of the mirror in his loft, the whole outfit had made his ego do somersaults.

So, he was disappointed, and then outright pissed that his new appearance's first reaction at work was the barely suppressed laughter of his class.

"Dildos!" he thought, infuriated.

Scowling his way through class until the bell rang, Dalton took to the corridor even before some of his students. With no class for second period, he often took an early lunch.

"Dalton, what's happened? Did you take a cool pill? Are you working on a theatrical production of *Happy Days* after school?"

With his dark shades on, Dalton had raced right past Principal Haywood Baynor, who had been lurking near an entryway to the school and enjoyed busting Dalton's balls even before his recent fashion transformation.

Whether he was insulting him or not, Dalton couldn't just sprint past his boss, a formidable, eccentric whose ties never matched his suits. Dalton was forced to pause and yet had no ready comeback.

"Principal Baynor, please don't make me tardy to lunch," was all he could come up with on the spot.

"Oh no, I didn't mean to slow you down, Mr. Coolster, please proceed to whatever hep and happening lunch plans you have scheduled."

Aggravated, Dalton was again uncharacteristically slow with a rejoinder.

"Sorry, you weren't invited. There's some sort of a dress code," was all he could toss back.

He then sped away furious, though still determined to stick with the new look. Women were noticing him. He had no concrete evidence as such, but he was fairly certain that the possibly Persian girl who had sold him the leather jacket was more friendly than she needed to be and had complimented him when he tried it on and there had been encouraging, even flirty smiles at the coffeehouse he frequented downtown.

"Whatever. Fuck everyone and the gangly old mares they rode in on!" he swore to himself.

Dalton found the public phone that was a couple of blocks from Venice High and rang Nathan.

"Hey there, Mr. High Roller. What's up with tonight? Were we doing that job you had mentioned this evening or tomorrow?" Dalton inquired.

"This couple is out of town for a full week. I made an appointment tonight to meet Slinky. Why don't I swing by your pad around one in the morning, we'll grab the spoils in Vernon and then head to Slinky's? Let's handle that next job tomorrow night. Should be a breeze."

Nathan had recovered his confidence and was under the impression that the cop showing up at his door had been merely happenstance. No one had staked out his place and there had been no follow-up from the police at all.

"Great. Works for me," replied Dalton.

He had one more phone call to make and had decided there was no use blowing off Leah because he actually wanted to see her. Their longstanding friendship was a solid reminder of the life he once led before everything went haywire.

"Hey," he said into the receiver of the pay phone he held a distance from his ear, as he assumed it was germy.

"Hey," Leah replied.

"Tonight, maybe we could hit up an old standby?"

"Oh, I was sure you were going to flake out. What do you mean? Bob's Big Boy?"

"Yeah."

"Great. I'm busy. I'll meet you there after work, late I guess, say ten o'clock."

That evening, Dalton took the 101 into the Valley and got off in Burbank, pulling into the large parking lot of the oldest, still standing Bob's Big Boy, built in 1949, on Riverside Drive. Once a flourishing chain of family restaurants across California and beyond (its specialty, the double decker cheeseburger), many of the Bob's had been suffering and closing. Though, the Burbank mothership with its giant statue of its mascot Bob, a chubby boy in checkered overalls brandishing a double decker burger, and its bright streamlined modern style, was still prospering.

Arriving before Leah, Dalton put his name on the waiting list and was seated after twenty minutes. He was confident that Leah would not stand him up, but was getting very hungry watching platters of burgers and fries zip by. It was then that he made the decision that he was going to let her know what he'd been up to. He could no longer hold it in. Leah would undoubtedly be shocked by his confession, but was trustworthy enough to keep it between them and would provide him some sort of advice. Regardless of her reaction, he had to get it off his chest and Leah was his longtime confidant.

As he debated ordering a chocolate malt to start, she arrived apologetically.

"I'm starving. Sorry, the restaurant was packed tonight and we fell behind during the rush and then I couldn't get away," explained Leah.

"No problem at all," replied Dalton.

Leah flagged down the waitress with a demonstrative wave.

"You're ready to order, right?" she asked Dalton.

"I'll get the double deck cheeseburger with fries and ... water," she ordered.

"I'll have the same and a chocolate malt."

"Coming right up," said the waitress.

"Now, George Washington on a pogo stick, what's with the leather jacket?"

Before leaving, Dalton had shaved and was not wearing the sunglasses.

"It's a leather jacket. I don't know what to say about it. I've gotten a lot of grief over it already," answered Dalton defensively.

"It looks good," said Leah attempting to sound a more positive note than she had the last time they had met at the jazz dive. "It makes you look more robust."

"Is that sarcasm? Does that mean anything?"

"I mean to say it makes you look more studly."

"Whatever. Let me just expire here in peace with my chocolate malt."

Bob's Big Boy not only served mega-sized shakes and malts, but each came with an additional steel blending cup filled with another large portion of shake or malt.

"You know what I really can't stand is when people write L.A. without the periods," commented Leah at random.

"Like on Dodgers baseball caps?"

"No, that's more of a symbol they've got going for them, not the best example. I mean, say something like LA Yogurt without the periods. That's so lazy and inaccurate."

"If I were to tell you a real plum of a secret, a doozy if you will, would you swear to keep it between you and me, even if it involved possible illegal activity?" asked Dalton, now dying to tell her.

"Holy Spicoli! What is it?"

"Do you swear on the grave of Oscar Wilde that you won't tell a soul?"

"Shit yes! So much build up. It better not be that you shoplifted the jacket, because if so, who gives?"

"It's a little bigger than that. I am going to need you to actually swear on something that has some meaning to you."

"You ass! Okay, I swear on my boyfriend's life!"

"But when he dumps you, then what?"

"That's the best you're going to get out of me. Your sure to be mediocre secret will be secure."

"Then, it's this. Over the last few months, I've been hanging out with Nathan a lot ... "

"I am not going to believe that you are homo lovers, not buying it. That big lug would not get busy with you. Even if he did like men, you would not be his preferred type."

"I think I'm as likely to have sex with him as you are, seeing as I'm pretty sure he doesn't go for the whole chic dork trend. But no, there is not even a smattering of homoeroticism to our friendship. Actually, we are a pair of burglars. We break into mansions and steal everything we can grab in the dead of night. That's the secret. You wouldn't believe how lucrative it is. I'm rolling in it."

"I am not able to process that. You are a burglar? You're sure you're not a little confused and maybe you're a bugler, like in a brass band. I'm sorry, it's just not registering with me that you and Nathan rob mansions."

"Since he was wearing short pants, Nathan has been thieving and now he pulls off heists like it's basic math. He showed me his trove of diamonds and criminy, it's worth millions. They're buried in a storage unit out in Sun Valley. And you couldn't imagine the sort of criminal jerkamabobs I've met in the last couple of months, like Harvey Pretzel, this ghoulish wax figure that owns a pawn shop in a place called Cudahy, who buys all the stuff and resells it for a massive markup I'm sure, and there's a Russian jewelry smuggler named Borislav, and a guy who I think was his brother, with whom I got into a full scale brawl. Nathan had to pull me off these two ass-wipes."

"That is astonishing," replied Leah wide-eyed, beginning to believe all that Dalton had just revealed.

"For the last two robberies, I went in on my own," continued Dalton in a hushed, excited tone. "Nathan picked the lock. In the last house, this old geezer that lived there looked like Mr. Burns from *The Simpsons*, but with a young-ish wife. I noticed a couple of photos of them. He had left a wallet in the drawer next to his bed and in the wallet and the drawer he had $3200 cash just sitting there waiting to be plucked. His wife had a few solid gold bracelets and some other snazzy jewelry and designer handbags. Nathan knows the value of all that stuff like he's a Beverly Hills housewife."

"Dalton, what have you gotten yourself into?" asked Leah, now horrified and with an expression of astonishment and anger. "You are talking about decades in prison when you get nabbed and they are going to catch up with you. And Dalton, let me tell you, you were not built to survive prison. There's a gang of hard-ass dudes in there that will boot you around like a Hacky Sack. Just please promise me, you'll stop, you'll not return any calls from Nathan, who's obviously a psychopath, and you will dispose of anything you stole, right away."

"I've really fucked things, haven't I?" replied Dalton, eyes watery. "But I'm so far into this thing, you have no idea. Everything you said makes perfect sense, except I can't just throw everything away. I've changed and not for the worse and it's because of everything Nathan and I have done."

"Dalton, you're delusional. You're stealing jewelry. That's not an accomplishment! You can't put it on your resume. You've become a hood! It's wrongful that you are robbing people and have somehow grown to think that that is acceptable behavior, stealing a woman's jewelry. You know I care about you. Please stop!"

Dalton gulped uncomfortably. He then ran to the bathroom, making it into a stall before yakking. He was shaking and feverish. The unveiling of his secret had not gone as planned, or rather there had been no plan except to tell Leah the whole story and succeed in getting it off his chest to someone he trusted.

A lifetime later, he returned to their table. Rather than waiting patiently for him, she had tore through her burger and was almost done.

"Sorry, I just had a talk with Ralph on the big white telephone in there. He didn't have much to say. He just made a flushing noise. I guess I am going to skip eating. Do you want my burger?"

"Pass, thanks. You're going to stop, aren't you? Please tell me you are!" Leah pleaded.

"At the moment, we've got too much going on. Eventually, it all has to end. What you said, it's the truth. I need to talk to him."

"I don't think it's a matter of having a word with Nathan. You need to completely divorce yourself from him."

Dalton signaled the waitress for the check.

"So, what was the real story with that French tart? What ever happened there?" asked Leah, sure that Dalton had been previously untruthful on that subject.

"Just what I told you," replied Dalton, not ready to disclose everything. "She was bad news. You called that."

The check arrived and Dalton picked it up.

"Please don't try and pay that with your marked bills. I'll get it!"

Leah yanked the check from his hand.

Peeved at the Man, Harvey Pretzel sat in the front of his store watching *Homicide* on TV, reliving the past week in which the Man had invaded his pawn shop and harassed him with impunity. It had all begun on a hazy Monday morning when two men had entered the store wishing to unload several fake Rolex watches, something clearly a little off in their sales pitch. Spotting them as possible cops at the outset, Harvey had told them he couldn't do business with them. But this had caused them to become rude and belligerent, getting a little too involved in the parts they had created for themselves.

One of the same cops had returned with a different partner the next day, in uniform, and they had questioned him and searched through all the merchandise in the front of his store for a couple of hours. Though they had discovered no evidence of thievery, as he was careful to keep all stolen merchandise hidden in the back, it had been a humiliating experience and a reminder of past rousts that had resulted in his doing time.

176 ~ ADAM BREGMAN

They had asked him a series of familiar questions and tried repeatedly to ruffle his feathers bringing up his past record. But all they needed was a warrant and they could rip through his entire store and bust him many times over. Now, he had to debate moving all the loot before the cops returned with a warrant if indeed they were planning to, but he had become so accustomed to the out of the way location and relative security of his pawn shop that he didn't have another spot readily available. No matter what he did, whether it was random harassment or not, they were evidently on to him and it put his whole operation in jeopardy.

It might have made some sense to curtail the criminality, at least for a short while, or go on vacation, but Harvey Pretzel had been at it for a long stretch and was incapable of taking a break. So, he had asked Nathan to meet him at his home in Downey, a twenty-minute drive east of the pawn shop, which seemed safe enough. He thought it was very unlikely that the police would stake out his house, though he had no evidence of the police watching him at all.

Still fuming, as he had been since the harassment, Harvey arrived home at 10:30 pm swearing under his breath at his adversaries. He pulled out a bottle of Miller Genuine Draft beer from the refrigerator, sat on the sofa exhausted from stress, debated turning on the TV, decided not to, lied down on his side and then struggled to remain awake. He had not been sleeping well.

When the doorbell rang, he had been sleeping lightly and it came back to him quickly that he had been expecting Nathan.

"Good to see you again, Harvey," said Nathan at the door. "I wasn't sure how or where you wanted us to unload. We've got everything in one box."

"Bring it right in the front," Harvey replied in a whisper.

Behind Nathan, Harvey noticed the same little twerp standing there from the last time they had met and wondered how and why Nathan employed this obvious chump. It had been a long while, but he had preferred the French girl with the curvy figure he had brought with him on one occasion.

Nathan and Dalton came into the living room, which resembled a cluttered pawn shop with a few pieces of scattered furniture and white carpet, and laid the goods out on a coffee table.

Rarely showing excitement, as it wasn't helpful in his profession, Harvey's shark-like eyes popped out a little when he spotted the flashy yellow gold bracelet with tiny diamonds.

In a drawer on the other side of the living room, he pulled out a high powered magnet, a loupe (a jeweler's magnifying glass), a small stone, and a scale and went to work on the bracelet.

The bracelet didn't stick to the magnet, so he took a look at it through the loupe and stated "18k, not too shabby."

To be positive of its legitimacy, he rubbed it against the stone.

"A piece like this, it's hot. I would need to have it melted down," he said weighing it.

"I can give you seven grand for it, that way there's a little profit there for me too," said Harvey.

"How about eight grand? After all, gold is gold," bargained Nathan.

"$7500," he said almost inaudibly.

"You got it."

There were several other gold pieces of jewelry and Harvey went through the same routine with each, settling on two grand for all the remaining jewelry.

While Harvey examined the condition of the Gucci and Stella McCartney designer handbags, Dalton began wandering around the large living room and studying it like it was a mu-

seum, taking note of the silverware sets, antique clocks, cande-
labras, and large wooden trunks. Picking up a Nepalese kukri
knife and removing it from its leather scabbard, Dalton and his
curiosity began to distract and agitate Harvey, who was easily
irritated.

"Could you not touch that?" demanded Harvey through
his teeth.

Dalton didn't realize Harvey had said anything to him.

"Could you put that down?" insisted Harvey, slightly
louder.

"What's that?" asked Dalton, believing Harvey had said
something to him.

Steam coming out of his ears, Harvey got up from what
he was doing, walked over to Dalton, carefully grabbed the knife
and scabbard from his hands and put it back on the wall where
it had been displayed held up by two nails.

"Do you normally go into people's houses and start taking things off the wall?" demanded Harvey, his gray mustache
and black eyebrows standing at attention.

"Usually no," said Dalton, collected and a little bit
amused.

"Listen, dipshit," said Harvey, his shark eyes piercing.
"When you have been around the block more than once, maybe
then you can come into my house and start poking around like
you're in an antique mall. Until then, why don't you stand over
there next to Nathan and not touch anything."

As he said this, some spittle went flying from Harvey's
mouth nearly landing on Dalton's jacket.

Dalton looked at Harvey in disbelief.

"Harvey, do you think we could get back to business
here?" asked Nathan, attempting to simmer things down. "Dalton's not going to touch anything."

"That's right he's not going to touch anything, if he
knows what's good for him," said Harvey, indiscernibly.

"For the bags, $300," said Harvey. "The Gucci one is worn."

"Could you give me $500 and we'll call it a deal?" asked Nathan.

"Can't do it," replied Harvey still flustered. "$300 is it."

"You got it," said Nathan.

Harvey disappeared into a back room and emerged with a thick stack of bills, which he counted out to Nathan.

Back in Dalton's car, Nathan handed Dalton three grand, only half of which he could fit in his wallet, the other half went folded into his other pocket.

"Not bad for a night's thievery, eh?" said Nathan. "It's like taking candy from a baby."

"Easy as pie," said Dalton. "But our luck is sure to run out at some point. You've got to admit that. I think I would like to call it quits. I'd like to retire from this racket while I'm ahead."

"Like hell! You can't fly off to Brazil on that," said Nathan perplexed by Dalton's sudden yearning to get out. "You could spend that effortlessly in a couple of months, then what? We've got one helluva good thing going, all tied up with a pretty pink ribbon. You can't quarrel with that."

"Yeah, but eventually the po po are sure to catch up with us. All it takes is one slip-up, right?"

Nathan gulped at the recent memory of the cop questioning him at his door, but knew he needed to keep Dalton close to his hip.

"Look, I need you Dalton. I'm not going back to doing this thing on my own. As a twosome, we've been killin' it, in spades. Tell you what, let's do this job tomorrow night, then we'll take a little hiatus, spend some of this dough we've made, hit up some bars together, meet some gals and such and then discuss what we want to do next. You don't have any issues with that, do you?"

"I guess I will agree to the one job," answered Dalton tentatively. "But after that, I think I'm going straight."

"Okay, when you have your head screwed on right, we'll discuss it."

Nathan and Dalton drove north on the 5 freeway through an industrial wasteland, quiet and contemplative.

~ 13 ~

EAST EDGEWARE ROAD

Entering the Academy Tailor Shop in Pasadena, Nathan placed the blue pinstriped suit he had recently purchased at a vintage clothing store called Jet Rag on the counter and rang a bell. In a few seconds, the proprietor, an elderly Filipino man named Joe Navarro appeared and gathered up the suit.

"Hello, good to see you again. Very nice suit!" exclaimed Joe, who was as amiable as they come.

"It doesn't quite fit," explained Nathan.

"Go try it on!" said Joe, gesturing toward a makeshift changing booth propped up next to an antiquated shrink wrap machine. Framed on the wall of the store was an autographed photo of Urkel, the bespectacled star of the TV sitcom, *Family Matters*, and apparently the one and only celebrity client of the tailor shop who had coughed up an autographed photo, for it was the only item of display gracing the store's walls. Nathan had glanced at the Urkel photo on every occasion that he had frequented the Academy Tailor Shop, the somewhat indefinable, old timey charm of the place and its owner attracting Nathan back to the store like a bug to bright light.

Upon leaving the changing room, Nathan stood before Joe in the sharp looking suit with sleeves that were an inch too long, while Joe went to work with his measuring tape and some pins.

"I can fix this right up. When do you need it by?" asked Joe.

"Doesn't matter."

"How about Tuesday?"

"That will work."

"It's a nice suit, a very nice suit!" repeated Joe.

"Thanks," replied Nathan. "It was only 45 bucks."

"Good deal!" said Joe in disbelief.

Nathan's discovery of the Academy Tailor Shop had come about because it stood on the same street, North Catalina Avenue, as two neat rows of elegant 1920s bungalow apartments separated with a courtyard and walkway between them and typical of old Los Angeles or nearby Pasadena. In the first apartment, on the left, lived Nathan's current gal pal, Phaedra, whose skin was as white as chalk; she had bleached hair parted on the right with a prominent purple streak and a vocation as a freelance journalist who covered paranormal happenings, conspiracy theorists, cults, and local oddities for a variety of art magazines, newsweeklies, and obscure book publishers, and this placed her squarely in L.A.'s presently vibrant alternative scene, of which Nathan knew nothing. As was often the case, he had picked her up at a bar, 3 of Clubs in Hollywood, where her friend's horrible band, Foam Eyebrows, had played, and where she had fallen for Nathan straight away while dominating much of their wide-ranging conversation about weird Los Angeles. Since then, Nathan had taken an atypical and substantive liking to her, finding her to be a stimulating companion, which threw him for a curve. Her big bag of tricks in the sack also left him bowled over. On one occasion, he had invited her back to his pad, something he rarely did with the ladies, and over the last couple of weeks, he found himself having imagined conversations with her as if she was there with him, when she wasn't.

Having no romantic proclivities, Nathan didn't know what to make of these new gooey feelings.

As of late, things had been, for the most part, dandy. He had come upon another job, a real darling, which he had discovered on his own without a tip from the travel agent, who provided the info for most of the places he hit. It had taken just a teensy bit of pressure to get Dalton to agree to accompany him and everything was set for that evening. The only troubling matter on Nathan's mind was that he had gotten wind that Harvey Pretzel had been busted at his store and was languishing in county jail. This meant he would need to acquire a new, reliable fence and that would be no jaunt in the park.

Strolling down the street to Phaedra's apartment, Nathan was confident that she was around.

"Oh, it's you," she said, opening the door a little startled.

"Expecting someone else?"

"I wasn't expecting you," she said, opening the screen door and kissing him on the mouth with her thin, dry lips, "but, it's a pleasure."

Causing unforeseen goose bumps, it was exactly the reception Nathan had sought.

Phaedra picked up a nearby cordless phone and quickly finished a conversation that she had been having, surprising Nathan by mentioning that he had just shown up and using his name, as if the other person on the other end of the line was familiar with him.

"It was my mom," explained Phaedra putting down the phone. "I told her about you. I hope you don't mind. She wants to meet you. Remember, my mom is a professional ballerina. She's an artist and a free spirit. I'm sure you'll hit it off. She's very easy going. My dad's another story. He's an insurance executive and kind of a jackass. You don't have to meet him. He lives in Fort Lauderdale."

"I'd love to meet your parents," replied Nathan untruthfully, as he had hardly ever met a girl's parents during his entire bachelorhood.

Noticing a burning smell, Phaedra then turned and sped off toward her apartment's small, somewhat attractive, grandma-style, wallpapered kitchenette, where some eggs had been frying.

"Do you want a burnt egg?" she asked.

"I was hoping to take you out to lunch," replied Nathan.

"Oh, you're a sweetie. I would love to, but I have a deadline. That interview I mentioned with V. Vale, the publisher and writer, who is responsible for RE/Search Publications, is due at the end of the day and I'm nowhere near through with it. Did you ever read the book, *Pranks*?"

"No."

She sprinted from her kitchenette to her desk and picked up the book.

"Borrow my copy. You've got to read this! It's essentially an encyclopedia of classic pranks by punks and artists, like Joe Coleman blowing himself up onstage. It's clever stuff, some of it sort of sick, I guess. Actually, I may still need it for my article. Borrow it when I am done."

Nathan had no interest in the book.

"Maybe we can hang out tonight," continued Phaedra. "There's this event themed around the Kennedy Assassination at Al's Bar, performance art, some bands, general bad taste, should be fun."

"I have plans with Dalton."

"Oh, too bad," she said, truly disappointed.

Nathan speculated if there was a way to get into Phaedra's pants before she returned to her work. It seemed doable.

Returning to the kitchenette, Phaedra carved out the burnt eggs from the frying pan, slapped them on a plate, poured herself a glass of water, sat down at a small diner style table and began eating.

"You're sure I can't get you anything?" she inquired.

Observing Phaedra digging into her eggs, Nathan's sex drive took a tumble and he realized he should probably exit and start considering preparations for the evening's burglary.

"I have to grab some things at the market. I was going to Granny's Pantry in a little while. If you're not doing anything, do you want to tag along?" Phaedra proposed.

Nathan considered if this was another fairly obscure L.A. stereotype, the invitation to spend time with someone while they tackled their busy schedule of humdrum errands. It wasn't the first time he had been asked to accompany someone while they did their grocery shopping.

"Frankly, I was just thinking about you and so took a detour over here to be in the vicinity of your general hotness for a bit, but I'll give you a call and we'll hook up this weekend," said Nathan taking a step toward the door.

"Oh, I have a little time, honey. You don't need to rush out. You could even hang out here while I'm writing, read a book or just relax on the sofa."

"Thanks, but I'm going to hit the road."

Phaedra stood up, wiped her mouth, bounded over to Nathan in the always hectic manner in which she moved, grabbed his white cheeks and kissed him almost violently.

The kiss sent a jolt through his body and he reached around her and grabbed her ass.

"I can't right now, hot sauce," she whispered flirtatiously rubbing her body against his, "but you know I can't wait long. Give me a call tomorrow."

Flustered, Nathan kissed her again, opened the door and departed.

Through the open door, Phaedra's keen eye spotted the familiar Chevy across the street with the Black man inside. She closed the door and sprinted to the front window of the tiny living room.

Phaedra was positive that it was the same car with the same man inside of it that she had noticed outside 3 of Clubs when she met Nathan and left with him, and then again a couple of nights later when they had had dinner at the old-school, red-sauce Italian restaurant, Miceli's in Hollywood. The same car had been parked in a handicapped spot at the corner, and the man inside had his head turned away from them when they walked by.

Seeing the man clearly through her front window, she considered, "It's got to be a cop following my lover boy."

Turning on her heel, she ran outside into the courtyard, spotting Nathan getting into his car at the end of the block. She looked at the Black man in the Chevy.

"Fuck it. I have to know what's going on," she decided on the spot.

She hurled herself toward the Chevy and tapped on the closed window, as Nathan pulled out and rounded the corner down the street.

Talbert lowered the window, irresolute of how he was going to handle his blown cover.

"You're following Nathan, I presume," said Phaedra to Talbert. "You must know who I am. I know he's into some funny business. The other night I overheard a conversation that he was having with his friend Dalton, who I haven't met. They were up to something, planning a robbery perhaps. Nathan has no idea that I overheard this conversation. He was hiding in the bathroom with his phone. Is he a thief?"

"I don't know what you are talking about, ma'am," replied Talbert, unconvincingly.

"Oh, please! I need to know what sort of fishy stuff he's up to."

Talbert stared straight ahead, seemingly ignoring Phaedra, but in fact deliberating hastily if she would be of use to his investigation or foul the whole thing up.

"If you let him know about me," warned Talbert sternly, "even hint at anything, you're aiding and abetting and could be locked up where the big, horny lesbos might mistake you for a lollipop. Understand?"

"I don't want to be dating a guy who is being tailed by the police! Didn't I make that clear? I just want to know what he's done. I won't say a word to him."

"Where was he headed?" asked Talbert.

"Shit. I don't know. He didn't say."

Talbert turned on the ignition of his car, pulling out of his parking space, with Phaedra in the middle of the street, stepping out of the way.

In a freshly nabbed silver Ford Explorer, Dalton and Nathan glided in the dead of night on to a very quiet Carroll Avenue in Angelino Heights, one of the few neighborhoods in the city of Los Angeles that still retained the adorned, vibrantly painted homes of the Victorian era, more common in San Francisco.

"That's it, the blue one on the corner," pointed out Nathan, "pull right up to that gate."

Nathan jumped out of the truck and lifted the latch on the heavy iron gate, as Dalton pulled the Ford Explorer into a side yard and then turned it around with the front of the truck facing the street, partially hidden by a couple of cypress trees.

"The houses across the street are practically staring us down," complained Dalton, as Nathan jumped back into the car to grab his bag of tools. "We're boxed in."

"There's no other way to do it," replied Nathan. "We can't load up on the street. If you see any lights go on in any of those windows, we're likely made and should book it out of here. Let me know right off."

Nathan exited the car leaving Dalton in the dark and out of his noggin paranoid. The suffocating terror that had been racking his brain since the fatal incident with Melanee had subsided for just a moment when Nathan had seemingly put things right. But it had come rearing back when he had succumbed so swiftly to a life of wanton criminality and only got worse after his confession to Leah and the realization of what he had done to his life. His fleeting confidence hadn't stuck. Now, it seemed, as he felt unable to break his bond with Nathan, that he had punched his ticket and it would be a tricky hurdle getting off the train before it went flying off the tracks.

Despite everything Nathan had said about being a professional, Dalton was pretty sure that they were coming for him, or if they weren't, they should be or would be eventually, and when they did, he had no real defense. At the moment, he was a jittery mess of nerves and sleeplessness. With every person that passed him on the street or said a word to him, Dalton felt he had plenty to conceal. The end was clearly arriving speedily and he only wished to hide in a dark room somewhere and for them to leave him alone. He wore his fancy sunglasses all day now, under the false impression that they might protect him from the glaring reality he faced. Around every corner, every time a door opened or the phone rang, they were dragging him away in handcuffs.

"Pop the trunk," whispered Nathan at the window. Dalton almost hit his head on the roof of the car, as Nathan dropped a heavy load into the back.

"The sword collection, it's huge," said Nathan. "I'm going to need you to give me a hand."

While cruising around the Angelino Heights neighborhood, to some extent innocently checking out the architecture, a couple of days earlier, Nathan had peaked through the window of the immaculate Queen Anne Victorian he was currently robbing and spotted several elaborate, bejeweled swords mounted on the walls. A little research online provided the name of the owner of the house, Edward Schiffer, an avid sword collector and dealer. The next evening, when he drove by the house again, this time to case it, several factors (the mail beginning to stick out of the mailbox and the lack of any cars around the house at night) signaled to him that no one was about and that he would have to move quickly, as he wasn't entirely confident that Mr. Schiffer was out of town, or if he was, when he might be back.

Entering through a side door that lead to a small guest room, formerly servants' quarters, then a hallway and finally to a vast living room, Nathan turned on his flashlight and whispered to Dalton, "Check this out."

The heavily adorned room was a museum-like, antique-laden stunner with embroidered hunting scenes next to stained glass windows and heavy blue velvet curtains, blue and gold Bradbury & Bradbury wallpaper covering the rest of the walls, a fireplace with a green marble mantle, cast iron seahorse andirons and a brass fan-shaped fire screen, a flowery green sofa with a giant Afghan rug between it and the fireplace, and a massive antique armoire, next to which there was an empty glass case on the wall from which Nathan had removed a sword.

"Upstairs," said Nathan, pointing to a creaky, narrow wooden stairway in the far corner of the living room.

They ascended and turned right into a large storage room, where swords were stacked on multiple shelves, both wrapped and unwrapped, some sheathed and some haphazardly piled on top of each other.

Snatching the older looking or more elaborately designed ones, they heaved them up and down the staircase, piling them in the truck.

On a whim, after a couple of times crossing paths with Nathan, who was almost twice as brisk as he, Dalton grabbed a thin saber from a shelf in the storage room and hid just to the side of the door waiting for Nathan to return.

"En garde," he said pointing the sword toward Nathan, upon his entering the room.

"Not the best time or place for swashbuckling," said Nathan, turning around.

"En garde," Dalton repeated, the ambivalence of his emotions regarding Nathan and his present ensnared situation swelling up inside of him in the form of a desire to act out.

Allowing that things were quiet and moving efficiently and that Dalton had been moody throughout the evening, Nathan decided what the hell and picked up a lightweight, un-adorned sword.

"En garde, you little piece of tripe," said Nathan.

Nothing was meant by Nathan's words, but it rubbed Dalton wrongfully and he lunged at him with his sword, which was parried by Nathan. The two then battled, Dalton forcefully, Nathan merely defending himself. For a friendly sword fight, Dalton's ripostes were a little too aggressive.

"Go easy," said Nathan, in the calming manner he some-times felt he needed to use with Dalton.

At one corner of the storage room, there was a small window partially covered by a stack of swords on a rack through which showed only a glimmer of moonlight. But as their oddly timed sword fight ensued, unmistakable red and blue lights shown through the window fuzzy and without accompanying noise.

With a tinge of terror in his eyes, Nathan turned toward the lights just as Dalton, still fixated on the sword fight, lunged planting the tip of his sword through Nathan's slacks and into his thigh just below his right hip.

"Holy crap!" cried Nathan.

Lowering his sword with its bloody tip, Dalton stood speechless, taking in both the wound he had delivered, as well as the even bloodier distress of their imminent capture.

"I didn't even realize the blade was sharp," was Dalton's dazed excuse.

"Thanks brother," replied Nathan, a grim, pained appearance taking over his features, his hand clutching his wound. "I don't know what's going on with you, Dalton, and I don't really care so much. I need you to focus now on us escaping in a silent and unseen manner. Got me?"

"Okay," answered Dalton, seeing no other way, ready to stick with Nathan out of sheer desperation, though he was without a doubt a tiny bit glad he had stabbed him.

With haste, they made their way down the stairs and to the slightly ajar back door, which Nathan peeked out of and slowly pressed open, as blood dripped down his pants leg. No sirens yet, only eerie silence.

"Stay here for a second," whispered Nathan. "I'll see if there is a way we can take the car with us."

Dalton wanted to say there was no way in hell, but Nathan was off. In a few seconds, he was back.

"There's a cop car in front of the gate. We're going to have to hop over the back fence and into the neighbor's yard," whispered Nathan.

Despite the wound, Nathan vaulted over the ornate, five-and-a-half-foot-tall, black, wrought iron fence with no trouble, while Dalton flailed at it like a turtle. Once over, they headed to a smaller side fence in the neighbor's yard and peeked down the side street, where a cop car was parked at the corner. In the dark, it was hard to tell, but it appeared there was no one in the car and Nathan made a facial gesture to Dalton to say that regardless, they had to bolt out of there. They hopped the fence and tore down East Edgeware Road, the neighborhood quickly changing from stately Victorian homes to scrubby stucco dumps. As they crossed the 101 freeway overpass, they heard a police siren and then a distant police megaphone. With cars buzzing by on the freeway below, it was difficult to make out the words, but Dalton believed he heard "Nathan Lyme," as well as his own first name, along with "cocksuckers."

"Is it possible that they know who we are?" thought Dalton, terrified and sprinting behind Nathan. "If so, the gig is up." He distinctly heard "Nathan Lyme." He wasn't certain about his own name.

Rounding the corner on Temple Street, Dalton shouted at Nathan, "Slow down for a second!"

Upon stopping, Dalton saw that Nathan's right pants leg was drenched in blood and he looked a mess: pasty white, perspiring profusely and not at all himself.

"Did you hear that?" asked Dalton, catching his breath.

"The police? Yes." replied Nathan.

"They said your name!"

"Really? Couldn't make out any of it. How could they have my name? You're positive?"

"Yes. I'm sure as God made little green apples."

"I don't know, maybe in the heat of the moment, you misheard. You've been an odd egg all evening, what with stabbing me and all."

"My hearing is fine. They said your name and I think they may have said mine."

"If so, our goose is cooked," said Nathan, attempting to slow his breathing and somewhat composed to a point. "They could tie me to the blood on that sword, no sweat. I shouldn't go home tonight. I've got somewhere else I can go. We need to split up."

Sirens wailed as Nathan spit out instructions.

"There's not much in the way of side streets around here that will take you downtown, where you could find a taxi in front of a hotel, so get yourself hidden if the cops come down here, which they will. I'll take off in the opposite direction. If you get collared, don't say a word!"

And Nathan sped away in the other direction heading west on Temple toward the spot from where the siren noise seemed to be coming. Dalton ran east seeing the 101 freeway underpass up ahead of him. He knew he didn't want to be caught on that underpass when the cops showed, but he hoped to make it downtown, where he knew the street plan. Before he could finish the thought, cop cars came roaring down Temple Street from Edgeware. The only person on the block at that hour, Dalton dived behind some trashcans hyper-ventilating. He believed the cops were far enough away that they might not have seen him. Indeed, they burst past him not slowing down. Still, if he wanted to make it downtown, it appeared as Nathan had said, that he had to run in the same direction that they had gone, so he did, but a little slower now, as the immediate area seemed quiet.

Crossing the underpass with only distant sirens and no traffic except on the freeway above, Dalton finally had a few moments to focus on the swirl of doom flooding his brain. For weeks he had known they were coming for him, and now he was in actuality on the run from the cops, lending credence to all of the paranoiac probabilities he had envisioned, wherein he was being interrogated with a bright light in his face trying but failing to deny everything, or he was in a dark cell attempting to read Dostoevsky under bad lighting, or he was walking into a communal shower butt naked and shivering with dread.

"How has it come to this?" he considered, as he made a right on Figueroa Street.

Everything pointed to Nathan.

"Not sure if it was worth it," he said aloud to himself.

On Figueroa, there was a little early morning traffic, so he stopped running in an effort not to stand out and instead walked briskly. He passed some large public health buildings continuing south along the desolate edge of downtown toward the business district, an area he was somewhat familiar with. As he came closer to 1st Street, a couple of pedestrians came into view, a nurse and a bag lady. He realized he was headed in the direction of his loft, though it was still a lengthy distance away, on the polar opposite side of downtown. No question, that was where he was going unconsciously since he had begun this odyssey. He could hide there in his darkened apartment with the shades drawn and never come out or only for work. The police would never invade this sanctum, he thought, none of his premonitions involved cops overrunning his loft. If he made it there, he was determined to drop his partnership in crime and his friendship with Nathan cold turkey. It was still very far, though, as he hoofed it up Bunker Hill on 1st Street, his feet and legs were now sore.

Passing the Dorothy Chandler Pavilion, where he had once, in a more tranquil period of his life, attended a classical concert with his parents, Dalton spotted an LAPD cruiser two blocks away from him heading south facing the opposite direction. He held his breath. There were no other humans in the vicinity. With nowhere to hide, he was a sitting duck. The cop car made its way very slowly down the street. He endeavored to walk as a normal strolling pedestrian would at five in the morning. The cop car was then out of sight down the hill.

"I can't expect another break," thought Dalton exhausted.

But there was another thorn poking at him. Once again, he considered, had he heard the police megaphone say his own name. If he had, he was toast. Dalton couldn't be sure.

Finally, he decided to take Hill Street south and passed Angel's Flight, the closed funicular that once ferried residents up and down Bunker Hill, when it was a crowded, working class neighborhood, up until the late Sixties. Dalton remembered that Nathan had been conversant about Bunker's Hill's rich history, as a location in numerous Hollywood films from the silents to the end of the black and white era and as a home to Charles Bukowski and John Fante and was particularly livid that the entire neighborhood had been demolished, in favor of erecting Downtown's modern skyline.

"It's a shame how things have taken a nosedive," thought Dalton, still conflicted. "I will never again meet anyone like Nathan."

Now, they were both in the soup, and Nathan was somewhere bleeding.

The sun rose, and with it cars and people appeared as if in a time-lapsed music video.

Dehydrated, Dalton stopped at a small taqueria at 5th and Broadway, which was serving breakfast at an early hour, and gulped down a large Pepsi. This normally crowded intersection downtown was beginning to come to life and Dalton conjectured that this was a chance to no longer stick out like a bug on a bench.

Stepping back onto the sidewalk, he looked east and with the sun now shining bright, he believed he saw Melanee at the end of the block.

"How can that be?" he wondered. "But the cut-off shorts, the dark hair, the curvy legs."

Cautiously, he walked toward her while preparing an apology for knocking her off a cliff to her death, as beams of horizontal sunlight obscured his sight. A guy on a skateboard sailed by him while playing a guitar. Then he passed a Latina lady in dark purple sweats. At the corner with her arm resting on a closed storefront, Dalton's vision was clearly not Melanee, curvy legs yes, but with a shriveled face and dead eyes. Having lived downtown for a few years, Dalton recognized the woman as a crack whore, perhaps younger than him, or older, it was hard to say.

As he stood there, two LAPD officers on foot turned the same corner and walked past him. One was a bulky, blond-haired cop with huge shoulders, the other a young and wiry Asian, who was staring at Dalton without pause as he went by him. Dalton turned his head, his heart skipping a beat, and the Asian cop had already turned around, having not taken his eyes off Dalton. He appeared to be reaching down, for a weapon or something else, and Dalton took off putting a block between them before the cops could react.

"Hey!" the Asian officer yelled and he and his partner gave chase.

"This is it, the bitter end," thought Dalton as he tore off now in the opposite direction of his loft.

Broadway, one of Downtown's main drags, with its reasonably priced stores catering to L.A.'s Latino population and shuttered, but once glorious movie houses, was rapidly filling up with people at this hour, all of whom stared at Dalton racing down the street with a solid lead on the two cops behind him.

One of the doors to Grand Central Market at Broadway and 3rd was half way open and with little time to think, Dalton burst through it, hoping that one of the back doors to the market would be open facing Hill Street. It was possible, he reasoned manically, that the cops weren't aware of the back doors and might proceed slowly thinking he was hiding somewhere. Dalton ran past the now deserted stalls, which in a few hours would be hawking meat, produce, and a variety of international lunch options, and found one back door that had also been pulled partially open, a cleaning crew standing nearby. They only had an instant to gape at Dalton as he soared by them.

Back on Hill Street, he ran south toward 5th Street again, where he had originally bumped into the cops, hoping this might throw them off. Peering quickly behind him, Dalton no longer saw them on his tail, so he dashed down 5th Street, ignoring the stares, still hoping to make it to his loft. But then there was a nearby police siren, more than one. Dalton tore down an alleyway. To the left, there was a parking lot, and Dalton found a hiding place between an SUV and a dilapidated pickup truck, where he was well concealed. Less than a minute later, a cop car came down the alley first speedily, then slowing down, as Dalton, sitting with his butt up against the large tire of the SUV, practically peed himself in fear. He could hear the two officers in the car talking to one another and chatter from their police radio, though he couldn't make out anything. But the car went by without stopping and then another cop car twenty minutes later did the same. The parking lot began to slowly fill up, but Dalton remained unseen.

After nearly two hours of hunkering down, Dalton struggled to stand up straight. The sirens had long quieted down. He looked in every direction and the coast seemed clear. Extreme exhaustion clouded with intense and unmistakably valid paranoia made it difficult for him to see or walk straight. He stumbled down the alleyway, arriving at 6th Street during the morning rush hour.

Returning to Broadway in a haze, he came upon one of Los Angeles' last cafeterias, the foresty, lodge-themed Clifton's, which had fed the down and out by the thousands during the Great Depression, and decided to grab a bite. After staring too long at the Jello, Dalton put a plate of apple pie with vanilla sauce and an orange juice on his tray and found a quiet spot on the second floor near a mounted moose head. Upon his first bite of pie, which tasted at this moment like one of the most satisfying things he had ever eaten, it occurred to him that he should be teaching class. This troubling thought had managed to secret itself in some corner of his brain while he had been thrust into a primitive kill or be killed pursuit with the cops, where survival had been all that mattered. Now his not showing up for work or calling in sick was nearly as traumatizing to him as his wanted status. He scarfed down the pie and hit the street, determined to call in sick when he finally got home, the only crappy excuse that he could come up with being that he had a fever and had overslept.

Several blocks down, he finally turned onto 9th Street and his heart began fluttering just a little bit with the anticipation that he would soon be able to sleep like a dead person. Stumbling onto Spring Street at the entryway of his loft complex, he practically walked into the three police cars parked at the curb.

"Dalton!" yelled Talbert whipping out his gun. "Get your dumb ass up against that wall there, arms and legs spread wide!"

Dalton succumbed, embarrassed, belittled, tears welling up.

Talbert read Dalton his Miranda rights, as a uniformed officer cuffed him behind his back.

"Please don't cry on me, you privileged white moron," said Talbert. "Obviously, we got you on breaking and entering, stealing a car. But what I've got to know is, was it you or your boyfriend Nathan, who offed this girl, Melanee Aston, threw her off a damned cliff?"

"It was me," mumbled Dalton. "I didn't throw her. I almost hit her and she fell."

"You're telling me it was just a little boo-boo then? What a shame," said Detective Talbert in the gleeful, showboating manner he sometimes affected in front of less experienced uniformed cops. "They sure don't make crazy white dumbfucks like they used to. What I am sayin' is you don't resemble the usual shit bag I got to deal with. I understand you teach high school kids?"

Dalton, still cuffed up against the wall of his loft complex, winced as a tear ran down his cheek, which he wasn't able to wipe away. Surrounding him on both sides now was an increasing pack of looky loos, a few of them familiar faces from the neighborhood, filling up the sidewalk, gawking. Dalton turned back toward the wall.

"Also, you're a tiny little man. I don't really get it. But you can explain it all to me, the whole fucked-up story, when we get back to the station. What do ya say? I'm a little bit interested."

Taking Dalton by the arm, Talbert led him to one of the police cars. In the next car over in the back seat window, Dalton saw Nathan's face, still pasty white, silently staring at him.

Dalton looked at him imploringly, wishing his friend had some last trick up his sleeve.

But Nathan's face said, "I got nothing."

Adam Bregman has spent an inordinate amount of time wandering around Los Angeles, where he was born and ran for mayor in 1993. He has written extensively for the *L.A. Times* and *L.A. Weekly*, covering every aspect of the city. He has also contributed to more than 40 publications including *The Stranger, San Francisco Chronicle, Boston Phoenix* and *OC Weekly*.

CPSIA information can be obtained
at www.ICGtesting.com
Printed in the USA
FSHW012015071020
74605FS